THE RED JUDGE

Also by Pauline Fisk for Bloomsbury

SABRINA FLUDDE

THE RED JUDGE

Pauline Fisk

First published in Great Britain in 2005 by Bloomsbury Publishing Plc
38 Soho Square, London, W1D 3HB

A CIP catalogue record of this book is available from the British Library

ISBN 0 7475 7160 0

All papers used by Bloomsbury Publishing are natural, recyclable
products made from wood grown in well-managed forests. The
manufacturing processes conform to the environmental regulations of
the country of origin.

Typeset by Dorchester Typesetting Group Ltd
Printed in Great Britain by Clays Ltd, St Ives Plc

1 3 5 7 9 10 8 6 4 2

www.bloomsbury.com

For Laura

CONTENTS

1

ZED FOR ZACHARY

I'll tell you when it all began. It was the day my sister Cary came home from her first term at university with a forty-watt light bulb superglued to the top of her head. I'd been out on a Christmas shopping spree, in a panic because it was the night of our annual Christmas party for my father's ghastly relatives, and I didn't have a clue what to buy for them.

Cary – I had no doubt – would have sorted herself out already with the perfect gift for every member of the family tucked away in her luggage. Not only that, but her train out of London would leave on time, and would arrive in Pengwern on time too. Trains always did, when Cary travelled on them. She was the princess of the family – a golden girl with golden curls to match, and brains as well, and a charmed life that ran as if by clockwork. If I'd been her, I would have stayed in London to avoid the party, but our father had persuaded her that it wouldn't be the same without her and she was actually coming home a day early.

Cary fitted in with the Fitztalbot family. That was the thing. She wasn't like me, who hated them. They didn't make her cringe. They didn't make her flesh creep. She didn't wish, like me, that she belonged to any other family. As far as she was concerned, they were all right as long as you worked out how to handle them.

But as far as I was concerned, they were the pits. I couldn't stand the way they stuck their noses into my life, always wanting to know what I was doing and suggesting ways that I could do it better. Or the way they swaggered around, thinking they were a cut above everybody else. They were an embarrassment. People in Pengwern bent over backwards to avoid them, but they didn't even know it. They were too busy boasting about their cars and houses and careers and children to see the effect they were having on anybody else.

And that was where I fitted in – or where I would have done if I'd only achieved anything to boast about. Unluckily for me, my father was the eldest son and, even more unluckily, I was his only son. In fact I was the only boy amongst the younger generation of the family. Anywhere else, this would have passed unnoticed, but it was a big deal to the Fitztalbots.

I was the one, you see, who was guaranteed to carry on the family name. The one upon whose shoulders hung the weight of history. The one through whom the Fitztalbot family name stood or fell, and they expected great things of me. But all I ever did was let them down.

'How's the dear boy getting on?' my father's sister, Aunt Decima, would whisper as if she thought I couldn't hear. 'How's his school work coming on? Are the grades any better? And the problems with the maths? Given the money you've poured into his education, I hope he's getting there at last.'

'Has he been selected for the team yet?' my father's brother, Uncle George, would ask about the rugby, cricket, tennis, badminton and rowing teams of which he had been school captain in his day. 'Well, never mind. Another term, maybe. There's lots of time yet. He's still young.'

The one who didn't skirt around the subject, however, was my grandmother. She was always direct and to the point. 'Is he pulling round at last, and behaving like a Fitztalbot?' she'd ask in a booming voice that was loud enough for the whole of Pengwern to hear. 'Such a lucky boy, to have his advantages in life. I hope he knows it. It could have been so different. He could have grown up in an ordinary family, never knowing any better. I hope you've told him how lucky he is. And I hope he hurries up and starts making something of himself!'

How to buy presents for a family like that? I mean, what would *you* do? In the end I bought a fart cushion for my windy uncle, a joke book for my humourless aunt, a collection of surprisingly realistic-looking plastic turds for my ghastly Barbie-doll cousins, Frieda, Lottie and Claudia the Clod, and a bag of lemon drops for my grandmother, who always looked as if she was sucking lemons anyway, her cheeks drawn in, her lips tight and her eyes watering.

For my sister Cary – who might have been the Fitztalbot princess but was still the nearest in the family that I had to a friend – I bought a nice silver ring with a turquoise stone. For my mother I bought a diary, because I couldn't think of anything else. And, for my father, I bought a print of Pengwern's old town gaol, hoping he would get the point.

Then last of all, but definitely not least, I bought a present for myself. It was a can of spray paint and, with it, I sprayed zeds all round the town. Zeds for me, Zachary Fitztalbot. I sprayed them anywhere that I could reach without being seen – down the medieval shuts and alleys in the wild west end of town; on the backside of an empty bus; even in the modern shopping mall, taking a risk because there were people about.

Finally I faced the supreme challenge of the railway bridge. I climbed up on to its girders – which was no mean feat, I'm telling you – and worked my way along until I was out over the river. Every time a train went over, the whole bridge roared and startled pigeons flew overhead, nearly knocking me off my ledge. But I clung on tight and, at long last, reached the middle of the river.

It ran full and fast beneath me, rippling with dangers that were known to every child in Pengwern. If I fell off my girder, I wouldn't stand a chance. There were hidden currents down there in those rushing waters, waiting to pull me under.

But I'd never been one to mind a bit of a challenge. In fact, I'd always seized the chance to give myself a fright. I was the sort of boy who'd lie awake at night, telling himself that he could hear the hounds of hell out there in the darkness, baying at the moon. The sort who'd scare himself silly watching horror films that no one else could bear, staring without blinking while his cousins hid behind the sofa, praying that their mothers would come and turn the telly off.

And I wasn't blinking now, high on the girders, spraying a massive blood-red zed on the central iron panel on the bridge. Then I stood back and looked at what I'd achieved, challenging anybody walking on the river path to see me. It was a good moment. There was something clean about it, somehow. Trains rumbled overhead but I stood undeterred, watching the river flowing out of town, wishing that I could go with it and leave my old life behind.

Just for a crazy moment, I imagined that I could – that it was possible to stop being a Fitztalbot and be some nameless boy instead. One who wasn't expected to be clever and do great things.

In the end, however, I gave up dreaming and went home. I had promised my mother to help decorate the house for our party, and I was late. I reached Swan Hill just as the streetlights came on. It was the grandest of Pengwern's streets, with all the biggest, oldest houses, and ours was bigger than the rest of them, set back behind cobbles. Iron gates swung open automatically when cars went in and out, but I slipped through a side gate, entering the house through a scullery door that led to a back staircase.

This enabled me to reach my bedroom before anybody saw any tell-tale signs of red paint. I changed my clothes, scrubbed my hands, and packed my presents quickly and clumsily, using lashings of sellotape. Downstairs, I could hear my mother moving from room to room, getting ready for her big night. She was famous for her entertaining, which always beat everybody else's hands down. I could hear the kitchen full of cooks, shipped in for the occasion, and the dining room full of waitresses laying tables.

When I'd finished with the presents, I took them down to the drawing room to slip under the Christmas tree. Here I found my mother decorating it with pinprick fairy-lights, strands of silver, velvet ribbons and a collection of priceless Venetian spun-glass baubles. For a moment, I stood in the doorway watching her. She was an older version of Cary – same cheekbones, same golden curls, same violet eyes.

Then she looked up and saw me, and the eyes clouded over. 'Ah, Zed,' she said. 'So you've finally decided to honour us with your presence! What time do you call this?'

I muttered something about crowds in town, and the difficulty of finding presents. My mother fixed me with a knowing look and said she hoped I hadn't been getting into trouble. I looked straight back and said I hadn't. Then, to change the subject, I offered to finish off the tree.

My mother shuddered at the thought of what my hands might do, especially to her precious spun-glass baubles. 'You know how clumsy you are,' she said. 'But you could go round the house instead with this sack of greenery. Decorate anywhere that looks a bit bare. And hurry up about it – Cary will be home soon.'

The unspoken word between us was that everything had to be perfect by the time my sister walked through the door. I took the sack and made off with it, hurling holly and ivy everywhere, bored before I'd even started. It didn't take long for the sack to empty. With just a few sprigs left, I sneaked into my father's study, which my mother had left out because he hated anybody going in there, even her.

My father's study was his *inner sanctum* – the place he went to get away from the whole wide world, including us. Even the cleaning lady wasn't allowed in there unless my father was present to supervise her movements. The only times I'd been in there were when I was in trouble, and he'd called me in.

Now I marched in recklessly and started chucking about my last few sprigs of holly. Even though I knew my father hated Christmas decorations, I still did it, climbing on to his desk to hang up a bunch of mistletoe and sending half its contents flying in the process. Notepaper, fountain pens, ink, pencils, diaries and even a couple of photographs crashed to the floor, the glass smashing in their frames.

One of them contained a photo of my mother, and the other a photo of Cary. I picked them up and threw them in the bin, along with the broken frames, knowing that I was in trouble anyway, and telling myself that I didn't care. Then I put everything else back, including a photo of my Fitztalbot grandmother, realising, with a little stab of pain, that my father didn't have one of me.

I looked around the room, but there wasn't one there either. My Uncle Henry was there, in his youth, and so was my Aunt Decima. There were even photos of Frieda, Lottie and Claudia, but there wasn't one of me.

Perhaps that was the moment when my life started changing. Perhaps it didn't happen when Cary walked through the door with that light bulb stuck to the top of her head. I stood looking round the room, feeling shocked by my discovery. I knew I shouldn't be, and yet I was.

Then I left my father's study without a backward glance, and returned to the drawing room. Here everything was as it always had been, and yet it all felt different. My mother was just finishing the Christmas tree, tying on the last glass bauble. It looked just like the trees you get on Christmas cards with Victorian families standing round them drinking punch.

'What do you think?' my mother said. She looked across the room and smiled at me, but I couldn't bring myself to smile back. It could have been a nice moment between us, but I wouldn't let it happen. And then the chance was gone for ever, and I didn't even know it.

The front door downstairs closed with a bang. Footsteps rang out on the hall floor and I knew they had to be Cary's. We both did. My mother turned away and I was immediately forgotten.

'Darling, we're up here,' she called, as her grade 'A' daughter's footsteps started up the stairs.

I waited for Cary to make her entrance, trying not to feel jealous, because I liked her, I really did. She couldn't help it if she was clever, and made my parents happy and was a credit to the Fitztalbot name. Her footsteps reached the top of the stairs and headed for the double drawing-room doors. My heart started pounding, but I couldn't have said why. Suddenly I felt frightened – and it wasn't the sort of late-night horror movie fear that I normally enjoyed. Not the sort I courted for the thrill of it. This was something else.

'Welcome home ...' my mother called, before the doors had even opened.

She moved towards them, but I moved away. Something was missing on the tree, I decided. Something wasn't quite right. I reached into the box and found a final bauble. I knew I shouldn't touch it, but I'd picked it up before I could stop myself, and then the doors flew open and Cary appeared. She was brightly spotlit, but I couldn't at first figure out why.

Nor could I figure out if she really was Cary! The voice that greeted us was hers, but how could my sister be this shocking person in army boots tied up with string, a black lace dress hanging like a rag, a face studded with chains and rings, eyes circled heavily in black, a coot-bald head with not a golden curl in sight and a light bulb, complete with battery-pack, superglued to the top of her head?

I dropped the bauble, which shattered into pieces.

'Really, Zed – you're so clumsy! Now look what you've done!' my sister's light, laughing, all-too-familiar voice said.

2

CARY COMES HOME

I gawped at Cary, my expression frozen. My mother gawped as well, as if she couldn't work out how this uncouth person had got into her house. You could see that she hadn't got it yet. See she didn't understand. Then Cary smiled the way she always used to do, every day when she came home from school.

'What's on the menu, Mum?' she said. 'It sounds as though they're busy in the kitchen. I'm so hungry I could eat an ox.'

Then, finally, our mother got it. Every hint of colour drained out of her face, and she had to grip the nearest chair. 'Cary?' she said. 'Oh my God, oh Cary, *no*!'

There was something terrible in her voice – something I'd never heard in her before, not even when I'd got myself expelled from school. I said 'No' as well, but there was a hint of a thrill about it, I'm ashamed to admit. For where was our princess now – the perfect daughter with the straight 'A' grades, who played the violin, sang like a bird, rowed for the county and always won? Where had she gone – and what were the Fitztalbots going to say when they arrived for their party?

And what would our father say?

Our mother sucked in her breath, as if trying to gather strength. Cary turned from her to me. There was triumph in her eyes as if she'd proved something. *What d'you think*? her eyes seemed to say. *I bet you never thought I'd got it in me to do a thing like this!*

And she was right. I stared at Cary, struck dumb, not knowing what to do. Should I laugh or cry? Cary did a little twirl, holding out the edges of her black lace dress. Our mother started weeping, tearlessly and furious.

'I don't *believe* it! Your beautiful hair! Your lovely face! Oh my God! Have you gone mad, or something? *What have you done?*'

Her voice grew louder as the words came out. Her eyes were popping and her face turning purple. I began to wonder if she was having a heart attack. Cary must have thought so too, because her bold smile puckered into a frown. You'd have thought she would have expected something like this, but she looked as if it was only just dawning on her that she'd gone too far. For a clever girl, it was amazing how dumb she could sometimes be.

'Don't take it so hard,' she said. 'Look, I'm sorry. I should have warned you. Please don't cry. It's not as bad as it might seem. My hair'll grow. The studs'll all come out. Even the light bulb will come off eventually. It was only meant as a bit of fun. A fairy-light for Christmas – that sort of thing. A decorated face, to go with your decorated tree. I did it for a laugh.'

'A laugh!' my mother spluttered. '*A laugh?* You'll laugh, my girl, when your father finds out what you've done!'

At the mention of our father, my sister's face tightened like a drum. Everybody in the household knew that our father was completely lacking in any sense of humour. There was only black and white with him, never any shades of grey. Only ever right and wrong.

And this was definitely going to be wrong.

'Maybe I could hide in my room until the party's over,' Cary said, looking at our mother and pleading with her eyes. 'You could pretend that my train was delayed, then break it to him gently when everybody's gone.'

My mother stared at Cary as if she was even madder than she'd first thought. 'You don't seriously think *I'm* going to tell your father what you've done?' she said. 'You do your own dirty work, my girl. You face this on your own. There's nothing, *nothing,* that I'm prepared to do to make it any easier!'

She swept from the room, gathering what remained of her composure and passing Cary without another glance. We heard her sobbing on the stairs. Her special night was ruined, and probably the whole of Christmas too. Not knowing what else to do, I took her up a glass of hot milk with brandy in it, and some migraine pills. My mother took them from me, but she didn't thank me. I don't think she even really saw me.

I left her crying in bed, and went downstairs to find Cary crying too, sitting on the window seat, looking like a sad clown who'd got the jokes all wrong. 'I've been an idiot,' she said. 'I know I have. I somehow thought I'd get away with it, but now I'm back, I can't imagine why. I've been a fool. But then I never would have done it if it wasn't for you. *I only did it because you bet me to!*'

This, unfortunately, was true. I sat on the window seat by Cary's side, staring into the darkness and trying to take in what I had done. It had all happened weeks ago, and I'd almost forgotten it until today. Now I cursed the evening when I'd picked up the phone, and it had been my sister on the line, going on about her new college life. She'd told me all about the exciting places that she'd been to, and the music in the clubs and the wacky clothes that people wore.

On and on she'd gone, as if she'd seen it all and I was just some baby-brother hick from sleepy Pengwern. Some of her new college friends had body piercings and tattoos, and she was thinking of having something done too. One of them even had a stuffed albatross superglued to the top of his head. I said he sounded like an idiot, but Cary was impressed.

'He's one of fashion's foot-soldiers,' she'd said. 'I admire him. I really do. Imagine being brave enough to go out looking like that!'

'I wouldn't call it brave,' I'd said. 'I'd call it stupid. All your friends are stupid, and so are you for going round with them. I mean, *an albatross*! Nobody in their right mind would do a thing like that.'

Cary hadn't hesitated. 'I would,' she'd said.

I hadn't hesitated either. 'Ten pounds says you wouldn't,' I'd said.

'*You're on!*' Cary had said.

And now she'd won. I'd thought that she was joking, but here she was, sitting next to me on the window seat, her hand outstretched, waiting to collect.

'You old stirrer, you. You've really done it this time, haven't you? You've really got me into trouble!' she said. 'Come on. It's payback time. The least that you can do is give me what you owe!'

I left the room, saying that I was going for the remains of my Christmas present money. But, no sooner were the doors shut behind me, than I fled. I knew that it was cowardly of me, but all I could think about was getting out before our father came home. Upstairs my mother was crying, and downstairs my sister's ugly, sad face was a testimony to what a terrible person I was. This was my fault and mine alone. Once the dust had settled, I was going to have to take the blame for it – but I wasn't ready yet.

I left the house and headed up Swan Hill, telling myself that I wasn't coming home until everybody had gone to bed. Christmas shoppers streamed past me, laden with their purchases, weary but happy. I had been like them only a few short hours ago, but now I pushed my way between them with only one thing on my mind – looking for somewhere to hide.

But Cary didn't let me get away as easily as that! Before I even reached the top of Swan Hill, I heard her voice behind me. She yelled at me to come back and, when I turned round, I saw her charging after me, light bulb and all.

Other people turned as well, and I pushed my way between them and cut down through a network of alleys, hoping that she wouldn't know them as well as me. She was a High Street girl, after all, not a spray-can troublemaker who spent half his life skulking down alleys.

Finally I emerged into the main town square, where a crowd was thronging round the town's main Christmas tree, and a band was playing carols. Only a few hours ago I'd been like these busy people, buying in a panic. But now that panic faded into insignificance. I couldn't imagine what I'd been worried about. A few stupid family presents – what did they count for?

I cut across the square, pushing my way between the crowds. 'Hey Zed, you rat – *wait for me!*' my sister called.

I turned round, and there she was, still behind me. The crowds parted to let her through, and everybody stared, just as they had done on Swan Hill. Cary was getting closer all the time, shouting for all to hear that I was a stinking pig and a filthy traitor.

'We're both in this together,' she yelled. 'You come home with me, *right now*!'

Later I was to wish I'd listened to her. Then my story would have turned out differently, and so would hers. But I was the sort of boy who always had to turn a little drama into World War Three. So I carried on regardless, promising myself that when I reached the shops on Pride Hill, I'd shake Cary off for good.

It was a stupid thing to do. But something got into me, and I was determined not to give up without a fight. Suddenly it was like those games of hide-and-seek we'd played when we were little. She'd been the older one, and cleverer by far, but I'd been the one who ran rings round her and always won.

Now I told myself that I could do it again. I cut across the High Street without stopping to look left into the oncoming traffic. And Cary ran behind me, without looking either, as if following me exactly was all part of the game. I reached the middle of the road and a small black car bore down upon me. For a split second, I froze, not knowing what to do. And, in that split second, the car swerved to avoid me – *and hit my sister instead.*

It missed me by a shaver, but it got Cary like a bull catching a matador in its horns. It's a sight I'll never forget. One moment she was right behind me in the road, then the small black car was going one way and Cary the other, flying straight into a bookshop window that shattered into pieces.

It all happened so quickly. Everybody screamed, and the traffic on the road screeched to a halt. A crowd started gathering, but the only person that I recognised was our father. His collar was turned up against the cold, and he held a black umbrella over his head. Under one arm was tucked a bag of Christmas goodies and, under the other, a bottle of champagne. Maybe they were gifts from grateful clients, or maybe he'd bought them to celebrate Cary's return.

Either way, we'd never enjoy them now – and neither would anybody else. The goodies fell from my father's hand, never to be seen again, and the bottle smashed all over the pavement. But he didn't notice. He was too shocked. His face was white as if, like me, he'd seen the whole tragedy unfolding.

Which meant that, like me too, he knew who was to blame.

3

ROWLEY'S RIVERLIFE MUSEUM

On ordinary days, Rowley's Riverlife Museum closes at five-thirty, but on late-night Christmas shopping evenings, it stays open like everything else in Pengwern, and the last visitors don't leave its museum shop until seven-thirty. Then the sales assistant closes it down, and the coffee shop too, and the curator goes round the whole building, pulling down blinds and drawing curtains. She shuts all the doors behind her, then moves through the building to the entrance hall where she sets the burglar alarm. The front door stands open and, in the time it takes her to nip into the cloakroom to pick up her handbag, anyone could slip in.

I know this for a fact, because that's what I did the night of Cary's accident. I tiptoed past without her noticing, and got myself locked in. It was a crazy thing to do, but seemed to make sense at the time. I'd been wandering round for hours, and it had started raining and I was soaked to the skin. I couldn't go home for fear of all the trouble I'd be in, and was even more frightened of going to the hospital.

So, needing somewhere warm where I could dry off – and somewhere dark, too, where I could bury myself away – I slipped in past the curator. She shut the door behind me, double-locking it from outside. Then her shoes went tapping down the cobbles, and I had what I wanted.

I was alone. Silence fell, along with all the darkness I could ever ask for. Immediately, I realised what a stupid thing I'd done. What if Cary called for me from her hospital bed, and nobody could find me? What if she died in the night, and I was stuck here unable to say goodbye? I imagined everybody around her bed – all the Fitztalbots silently blaming me for what I'd done to her. I had made things even worse – what a fool I was!

I went from room to room, lifting blinds and looking for a window to get out through. But all of them were locked, and so were the fire exits, and the kitchen door, and the museum office where I'd at least hoped to find a phone.

I banged on the front door, shaking it on its hinges, and jumped up and down in the hope that I'd somehow activate the burglar alarm. But it stubbornly refused to go off, and I tried shouting through the letterbox instead, and running through the building, banging on the windows and calling for help.

But nobody heard me. Rowley's Riverlife Museum is situated in a quiet part of town between trees and empty office buildings and, even when I switched on all the lights, there was nobody to see.

So much for police protection of public buildings, I thought. So much for town centre closed-circuit TV, and neighbourhood watch, and everybody being on the lookout to beat crime. I'm stuck here and, by the look of things, I'll stay this way until morning.

The lights went off again, on a timer, and I was plunged back into darkness. Deciding to make the best of things, I helped myself to biscuits and milk sachets in the coffee shop, and a plaid rug 'woven from Shropshire wool' in the tourist shop. Then I made my way through the building looking for somewhere to sleep or, at the very least, make myself comfortable.

But that was easier said than done. Once Rowley's Riverlife Museum had been a merchant's mansion, teeming with warmth and activity – a grand Tudor family house, as full of life as a walled city. But where there once had been huge old fireplaces and four-poster beds, now there were information boards and display cabinets, paintings and photographs, stuffed fish and birds, models of flat-bottomed river boats called trows, old maps, old fishing nets, long eel baskets called putcheons and nastily pronged eel forks that looked like the devil's own favourite weapon.

There wasn't even anywhere to sit down. I did find a coracle in the Sabrina Room – dedicated to Pengwern's queen of rivers, known commonly as the River Severn, but locally, as the Sabrina Fludde – but it was a fragile-looking thing that could be hundreds of years old, and I was afraid of breaking it.

In the end, I curled up against a storage heater in the Wye Room, dedicated to the river that Grace, my other grandmother, had always called by its Welsh name, the *Afon Gwy*. I'd always thought of it as her river because her house looked down on it, and perhaps that's why I chose it now.

I huddled against the storage heater, looking up at an old painting of the Afon Gwy, remembering swimming in that river and watching Grace fish. Not much had changed since that picture had been painted, as far as I could see. The river still flowed down from Plynlimon Mountain on exactly the same course, and the valley was just the same, winding between great flanks of hills that rose to hidden summits.

The only difference was that Grace had gone. She was dead, I mean, struck down in her garden pegging out her washing, with not a hint of a warning that a heart attack was on its way. It had happened a year ago now, but I was still trying to come to terms with it. As much as I had always hated my Fitztalbot grandmother, I had adored Grace. Now, with her gone, there was nobody to stick up for me, getting on the phone to tell my mother to go easy, and refusing to hear a word against me, no matter how much trouble I was in.

Not that she could do that now! If Grace were still alive, I thought, there'd be nothing she could say this time. What was there to stick up for?

What indeed? In my mind, I played the whole thing through again. It started with my sister standing in the doorway, and ended with the ambulance taking her away, with my father clinging on to her. You could see from his eyes that he didn't know a crowd was watching. All he knew was what he'd seen – Cary getting hit and me, who'd led her out into the traffic, getting off scot-free.

Except that I hadn't got off scot-free. I'd done something terrible and here, curled up against the storage heater, shivering in my soaking clothes, I knew that life would never be the same. Everything, *everything*, was my fault. How many times had my mother said, 'If you carry on like this, my boy, you'll get yourself into *real* trouble one day.'

And now I had. In the darkness of that cold museum, I was haunted by her words. They picked at me like goblin fingers, making me afraid. It wasn't the sort of fear that I'd once enjoyed, either – the sort I'd felt when spray-can painting on the railway bridge or watching scary movies on the telly. I couldn't just shiver, and laugh, and live to tell the tale another day. Here in Rowley's Riverlife Museum there *was* no other day. I was trapped in the darkness, alone with my thoughts. I couldn't shake them off.

I reached for the plaid rug, and pulled it round my shoulders, but couldn't stop shivering. Cold-eyed gargoyles from some ruined Wye-side abbey glared down at me as if they knew what I had done. Old fishermen and riverboat men glared down, too, from their photographs on the walls. Their faces seemed to condemn me, as if they all knew what I'd done. I felt on trial, with nobody to defend me and not a word that I could say on my behalf.

Even the *Cŵn y Wbir* looked down at me – Plynlimon's legendary hounds of hell whose hunting grounds were the skies above the mountain. I hadn't noticed them before, but now I could see them in the painting of the Afon Gwy, and see their master too, the famous Red Judge of Plynlimon who – as every child knew – would 'get you' if you were naughty.

And I'd been naughty, all right. I'd been more than naughty, and it seemed to me, looking at the painting, that the red judge knew it too, standing on his mountain holding up the black corph candle, that only ever burned for a death.

Guilt does funny things to you. In the morning, there were no candles in the painting, nor was the red judge in it, nor his *Cŵn y Wbir*. It was good to wake up and find myself lying on a cold, hard floor beneath a painting that had nothing in it but mountains, hills, a river and a few sheep.

I sighed with relief, and would have dropped back to sleep if a door hadn't sudden banged shut somewhere. Footsteps rang out in the big main hall and I heard a rattling sound – chains or keys, or something like that – and the beeping of the burglar alarm being switched off. Then voices started chattering, and I realised that a radio had been turned on.

I crept out on to the landing to see what was going on. Downstairs in the hall, a man in overalls was hauling a heavy-looking industrial-sized polisher across the floor, heading in the direction of the stairs. He was the cleaner – and he was coming my way. I looked around for somewhere to hide, and managed to get behind a door before he reached the top of the stairs. He passed me without noticing and, the moment I heard his polisher whirring in one of the rooms, I made my getaway.

I headed down the stairs and across the hall. The front door was still locked, so I turned towards the kitchen door instead. This was open, and through it I could see a vacuum cleaner and a microwave, plastic buckets and detergent bottles, mugs, a kettle and a big jar of instant coffee, all lit by a fluorescent strip-light.

I could also see the back door – which was open too, and led into a narrow alley where the week's rubbish had been lined up in black plastic bags. My escape route at last! I leapt over the bags and made the quickest exit possible, not even stopping when I tore one of the bags open, strewing its contents halfway down the alley. I was out of there, and no looking back – on my way home, ready to face whatever I was in for when I got there.

I couldn't get home quickly enough. But when I slipped through the side gate, the house stood in darkness as if none of us lived there any more. It looked abandoned, and a shiver ran through me. I let myself in, telling myself that everybody was asleep, and that was why the lights were off. But my parents' bedroom was empty and their bed unslept in, and the rest of the house was empty too. I went up and down every staircase, and in and out of every room, including the laundry room and even the cellar.

But nobody was home, and there wasn't as much as a note to explain what was going on. In the dining room and kitchen, I found tables and work surfaces laden with untouched food and, in the drawing room, I found the remains of the Christmas tree bauble that I had dropped, still not cleared up.

Obviously everybody was at the hospital – and that was where I should be too. I ran upstairs to change into some fresh clothes. On my bed were strewn the wrappings of the presents that I'd bought the day before. I stared down at them, remembering another world where joke books had seemed funny, and plastic turds a good idea. Now that all felt so long ago.

Suddenly my thoughts were interrupted by the sound of crunching on the gravel outside. It stopped beneath my window and car doors banged. My mother called something to my father, but I couldn't hear what. I heard them entering the house, their footsteps ringing in the hall. Then they started up the stairs, and the hairs rose on my head. I remembered the candle burning in my imagination – the black corph candle burning for death – and prepared myself for the worst.

But my parents passed my door and carried on to their room. They didn't even check that I was home. Through the wall I could hear their voices murmuring to each other, but I couldn't hear what they were saying. Glasses chinked as they helped themselves to stiff drinks. Then I heard them on the phone, passing on their news to everybody in the whole wide world, it seemed.

Everybody except me.

4

AT THE HOSPITAL

I hid in bed, pretending to be asleep in case my parents came in. I didn't want to find out what was going on, not any more. There was something grim about the voices through the wall – something about them that frightened me. I didn't want to know what had happened to Cary, and lay with my eyes tightly closed every time anybody went by.

But I needn't have worried because nobody came in.

Later, I heard my parents leave again. The front door slammed behind them and immediately I knew that I'd made another mistake. I leapt out of bed and ran to the window, wanting them to come back. I even leant out to shout at them, but it was too late. The automatic gates swung shut behind them, and my parents' car disappeared from sight.

I was alone again. I stood at the window, watching people passing down the hill. The rest of life – including Christmas – was still happening for them, but not for me. Sleet began to fall, and the day began to darken. I knew what I had to do, but couldn't find the courage. I stood like that for ages, wasting precious time – Cary's time as well as mine. Then, in the end, I phoned for a taxi, knowing that if I didn't go to the hospital and find out what was going on, I'd never forgive myself.

All the way there, I sat with my head down as if I was ashamed of anybody seeing my face. Pengwern passed by in a daze. In no time at all, we were on the outskirts of the town, turning into the collection of modern buildings and old Nissen huts that comprised the county's prime hospital.

The taxi pulled up outside the main entrance, and I paid my fare, still not looking at the driver. Then he drove away, and I was left standing in the biting cold with sleet blowing into my face. With a growing sense of dread, I hurried through sliding glass doors into a reception area where rows of chairs were filled with people who all looked about as happy as I felt. A massive vase of flowers stood on a plinth. The place reminded me of a funeral parlour.

I turned round, and would have left again if the woman behind the reception desk hadn't seen the state that I was in, and called out, 'Can I help you, dear?'

I asked where Cary might be found, and she tapped my sister's full name, CARIEDWEN ELIZABETH FITZTALBOT, into her computer and came up with Intensive Care.

'It's on the third floor. There's a lift at the end of the hall,' she said, pointing the way.

I went down the hall, feeling more reluctant every step I took. I had always hated hospitals, with their sense of secret sorrows behind closed doors, and pent-up fears. And now I had my own share of those fears and sorrows. I reached the lift and pressed for UP. A pair of stainless steel doors glided open with a 'ting'. The lift was empty and I got in, pressed the button for the third floor and listened as a metallic voice announced, '*Mind the doors.*'

Then the doors glided shut, and the lift rose for an eternity, during which it seemed to me that the light reflected in its shiny steel came from hundreds of corph candles. I knew it didn't really, of course. But it was a relief, all the same, when the doors finally 'tinged' open and I was released into Intensive Care.

I stumbled out, feeling lost, without a clue which way to turn. Signs hung over my head, with arrows pointing in every direction. I tried to work out which of them to follow, and suddenly saw my mother through a pair of swing doors. She looked just about as lost as me, standing in the middle of the ward, her usually immaculate appearance shot to pieces. Her hair was all over the place, she wore not a hint of make-up, and the expression on her face suggested that everything she'd ever worked for had been swept away.

At the sight of her, I felt my legs turn to jelly. I don't know what I would have done if she hadn't suddenly looked up and seen me. Our eyes met, and I knew I couldn't let her know how lost I felt myself. I marched through the swing doors, a stupid smile stuck all over my face.

'How's Cary? Is she all right? Can I see her? Where've they got her? Is she coming home soon? What do they say? Are they going to keep her in? Can I talk to her?'

That's the sort of stupid thing I said. But then I saw

the rest of them – all my Fitztalbot relatives clustered like carrion crows in the lounge at the bottom of the ward. They looked up at the commotion, and saw me, and my father looked as well.

He was sitting by Cary's bed, holding her hand as if he'd never let go. His face tightened at the sight of me. It actually tightened, like the skin of a drum, and my mother took his arm, as if to try and calm him down. He looked as if he was going to leap up and hit me, but she whispered in his ear and drew him down the ward out of earshot.

They went into the lounge together and shut the door behind them, as if the last thing they wanted was to have to look at me. I was left alone, standing in the ward. I went and sat by Cary's bed, taking my father's place. All around me lay trolleys and machines, winking lights and miles of tubing. Things blinked and bleeped and dripped, and I didn't have a clue what any of them were doing. All I knew was that my sister lay in the middle of them, her mouth full of lumps of plastic that were presumably doing something good for her, her head covered in bandages, her neck encased in a high yellow collar and the backs of her hands covered in fine little tubes. All the life seemed drained out of her – all signs of who she really was, completely disappeared.

'Oh Cary,' I said, as if the words were being dragged from deep inside of me. 'Cary, come back! You've got to. Cary, *you must*!'

At the sound of my voice, a nurse looked up from her desk. She was a busy woman, but her eyes were full of sympathy. 'That's good,' she said. 'That's what she needs. Talk to her. Let her hear your voice. Let her hear she's not alone. She mightn't answer back, but that doesn't mean that she can't hear.'

She bent her head again and got on with her paperwork, as if she didn't want to intrude on my private grief. I wanted to ask if Cary was going to die, but didn't dare. I looked at the bed and wanted to take my sister's hand, as my father had done. Wanted to feel her warmth, and reassure myself that she was still alive. But I didn't dare do that either.

In the end I pulled the chair up as close as I could get. Then I poured out my heart:

'I am so, so sorry,' I said. 'Everything's my fault. If anyone should be hit by a car, I'm the one! I never should have run out into the road like that. I mean, I knew that you were right behind me. I should have thought. And I never should have been out in the town anyway. I never should have left you in the lurch. It was cowardly and cruel.

'But worse than that – worse by far – oh Cary, *I never should have made that bet!* Will you ever forgive me? None of this would have happened if I hadn't challenged you! You never would have done any of it – shaved your head, or done that stupid light bulb thing, or the face piercings or anything, if I hadn't talked you into it. I know it's all because I goaded you. Oh Cary, please forgive me. Cary, *please live*!'

Cary didn't move. It was impossible to tell if she'd heard a word that I'd said. But someone else had. I heard a sound behind me, and turned to see my father standing halfway down the ward. For a moment we stared at each other. I didn't know where my mother was, and neither did I know how long he'd been there.

Nor how much he'd heard.

'I d ... didn't mean ...' I stuttered. 'I just said ... I was just trying ... I mean ...'

My father held up his hand. 'Come with me,' he said. 'What your sister needs is peace and quiet. We don't want you upsetting her. *Let's get you out of here.*'

5

BANISHMENT

We left the hospital together. My father gave no clues as to what he'd heard, but I was in trouble and I knew it. We walked in silence to his car, which he unlocked with a sharp stab of his keyring. We got in and I expected him to start on at me straightaway. But instead he turned the ignition key and put the car into gear.

'Are we going home?' I said, with some surprise.

My father didn't answer, just drove out of the car park, paying the parking fee in the box at the barrier. Sleet was blowing across the road in front of us, and hospital visitors were struggling with their umbrellas. Our car forced its way between them, almost causing an accident. We reached the main road and shot off way over the speed limit – heading out of town.

'Where are we going?' I asked as roads and houses disappeared from sight, to be replaced by fields and trees.

Still my father didn't answer, just looked ahead. His eyes were fixed on some distant point beyond the windscreen wipers, and his hands formed two tight fists around the driving wheel. We reached the bypass that marked the outer boundary of Pengwern, and he shot across it without even slowing down. The lights of town fell behind us and the sleet started turning to snow, running down the windscreen and gathering at the bottom.

I asked again where we were going, but still my father wouldn't tell me. He fiddled with the radio channels until he found some music, which he turned up loud so that we wouldn't have to talk. By this time, I was shaking and couldn't stop. I didn't like this. I didn't like it at all. My father had always been a difficult man, easy to anger, but I'd never seen him quite like this. Over the years I'd landed myself in all sorts of trouble, but he'd never gone silent on me. In fact he'd always had plenty to say!

Now, however, I was in new territory. I glanced at my father's face, not knowing what to expect next. 'Please,' I said, because I had to say something, even if he didn't want me to. 'I know you're mad at me, but can't we talk?'

My father didn't answer. He didn't say a thing or even look at me, just turned up the music. The weather was getting worse, but instead of slowing down, he drove faster. It was as if he hadn't noticed the storm that was developing, or how treacherous the road was, with snowdrifts blowing across it and more snow on the way.

Finally the music stopped, and some awful Christmas round-up programme came on instead. Normally my father would have turned it off, but he let it drone on. I don't think he noticed it any more than the treacherous weather conditions. He tore through villages and towns, over hills, past fields filled with snow, in and out of wooded valleys, on big roads, little ones, dual carriageways and country lanes. And I don't think he noticed any of it.

'Look, I know I've made you angry. I know it's all my fault. But can't we slow down?' I pleaded. My father was seriously frightening me by now. I cursed myself for ever going to the hospital, and even more for opening my heart to Cary. Plainly, my father had heard every single word of my confession. What had I been thinking of?

'Look, you've got to listen to me,' I tried again, afraid of making things worse but knowing I had no choice. 'I didn't mean to bring all this on Cary. I'm really sorry. I never in my wildest dreams thought it would come to this. I love my sister. I really do. You've got to believe me. I mean it. *Honestly.*'

My father looked ahead, as if contemptuous of my honesty. He drove even faster than before, and I knew that I shouldn't have spoken. On the radio, the terrible Christmas programme ended, and the news came on. Its wars and political rows seemed like nothing compared to what I was going through. I stared out of the window, with not a clue where we were. 'BOY ABDUCTED BY FATHER,' I imagined the newsreader announcing in the next day's headlines. 'TRAGIC FAMILY LOSES BOTH ITS CHILDREN.'

By now day was turning into night. The road was slippery with ice but still our car screeched round every bend we came to. My stomach turned over, but my father seemed immune to any sense of danger. I feared that he would kill us both. Imagined the car rolling over on this empty road, and the headline 'BOY AND FATHER KILLED IN TRAGIC ROAD ACCIDENT.' That's if anybody found us, of course!

By now the snow was thick on the ground, a shroud of whiteness covering everything. I shook my father's arm – then wished I hadn't as the car veered across the road.

'Slow down!' I yelled.

We careered round a bend, and missed a ditch by inches. I threw my hands over my head, and could scarcely believe it when the car righted itself. It didn't seem to me that my father had anything to do with it. His hands still gripped the steering wheel, but his eyes were fixed so far ahead that I could have sworn he didn't even see that bend. But at least we came out alive.

We carried on as fast as ever, the car slipping and sliding on the road like a beast out of control. Great hulking hills loomed over us, but I didn't recognise them. As far as I was concerned, we could have been anywhere in that long border country that stretches down from Pengwern. There was nothing special about the landscape that we passed. Perhaps it was the snow that made it so anonymous, or perhaps fear made it seem like that. Perhaps, even if I'd driven back over the Welsh Bridge, I wouldn't have recognised anything.

But, finally, I did. We pulled off the main road and started down a lane into a village that looked like a Christmas card, complete with glitter for snow. I caught a glimpse of houses with curtains drawn and others with decorated trees in their windows. We passed a chapel on one side of us and a shop on the other, a pub, a school, another pub and a row of cottages built into a hillside. Slowly it began to dawn on me that this wasn't just a Christmas card scene, but somewhere real that I actually knew.

We started slowing down. Ahead of me I could see an old church tower that I recognised, its stubby little spire standing dark against the snowy night. My father turned down the lane next to it and I saw a river with a bridge that I recognised as well, and a couple of cottages. One of them was almost entirely covered in scaffolding, and no lights shone from its windows. A builder's sign leant against the front wall. A concrete mixer stood in the garden. A FOR SALE sign was fixed to the gatepost, and I stared at it and understood at last what this long journey had been all about.

My father drew up outside, and I didn't need the name on the gate, Prospect House, to explain anything. He loosened his grip on the steering wheel and leant back with a sigh. Silence hung between us. I looked around and, sure enough, the pub at the end of the lane was the Black Lion Hotel, and the old church was St Curig's. If we'd carried on past it, we would have ended up on the pass road over Plynlimon, heading in the direction of the coast at Aberystwyth.

But we hadn't carried on. We were here – outside Grace's house. I stared up at its windows as if expecting to find her here as well. But the windows were empty: no curtains, no pots of plants and no ornaments. There were no lights either, even in the porch where there always used to be one. Once it had been full of logs, old newspapers and buckets of coal, but now it was so full of snow that I could hardly even see the front door.

I sighed as well. The last time I'd been here, I'd said goodbye for ever. Now here I was again.

'*Out you get!*' my father said.

It was the first time in our journey that he had spoken. Before I could do more than unlock my seat belt, he leant across, threw open the passenger door and booted me out on to the road.

Then he drove away.

6

PROSPECT HOUSE

The time has come to own up about something. I really don't want to, because there are things one doesn't ever want to talk about, and this is one of those for me. But there's no way that I can carry on without explaining why my father treated me the way he did that day.

Perhaps it's obvious. Perhaps I'm pointing out what anyone with half a brain could work out anyway. But the man I call my father isn't really. My real father, I mean. He adopted me. My real father died when I was a baby. I can't even remember him, and my earliest memories are all of Grace. My real father was her son, you see, and in those early days before my mother married again and my Fitztalbot father adopted me, Grace was my family.

Grace and Cary, I should say, because Grace brought her up as well, and the shock of adoption hit us both together. But Cary went quietly, while I made a fuss. A massive fuss, I might add, which I'll never forget, and I don't suppose anyone who heard it, right here on the road outside Prospect House, would ever forget either.

Perhaps it wouldn't have been so bad if the whole thing hadn't been so unexpected. But it came out of the blue – my mother turning up like that without a word of warning, and a new father waiting in the car outside, and a new life waiting in Pengwern; one that I didn't want because I thought the old one was just fine.

Cary didn't want it either, but she pretty quickly saw advantages in the situation that were beyond me. She missed Grace, of course, and the old days in Wales, but that didn't stop her settling in. She was everything our new father wanted in a daughter of his own. She belonged, right from the start.

But I was always an outsider. The Fitztalbots were never my real family, and I didn't want them to be, either. I rejected them long before they rejected me. And it all started on the road here, outside Prospect House.

Now I stood staring at the house, remembering my parents driving me away, in tears. I never forgave them for what they did that day, and I know Grace didn't either. The atmosphere was positively Arctic after that. When Grace died, Prospect House was left in trust for Cary and me. Not a penny of its sale was to go to our mother. Grace never visited us in Swan Hill, and whenever our mother took us down to Wales, you could feel Grace holding back her fury, as if she didn't dare to let it out. It was as if my mother had a hold on her – as if she'd got a trump card up her sleeve.

And that trump card, I grew to realise, was us

grandchildren. We only ever saw Grace when our mother allowed us to. This usually only occurred when she and my father went off on holiday, leaving us behind, but it was a privilege that could be withheld if Grace didn't toe the line.

'Be good,' our mother would call as she drove away. 'I'm trusting you. Only the very best behaviour. *You know what I mean.*'

I didn't know what she meant but I guessed that Grace did. She'd button up her mouth, and if looks could kill, my mother would be dead. But at least we were back. Even Cary would be pleased, and I'd be almost sick with excitement. Maybe it wasn't quite the same as living here full-time but I didn't care. Maybe we were seen as 'different' in a village where we'd once belonged, and some of our old friends couldn't understand us because our accents had turned English, but it was still good to be back.

'Cary might be English,' I told myself. 'She might have taken to her adopted country, but I'm still Welsh and proud of it. My father may pray for England when the rugby comes on telly, but I pray for Wales. As far as I'm concerned, it means nothing to be a Fitztalbot, and everything to have Welsh ancestry.'

It also meant everything to be Grace's grandchild. Unlike my Fitztalbot relatives, she was fun. She'd always have a go at things, and lived life to the full. She didn't mind making a fool of herself, and never bothered about stupid things like 'setting a good example' or 'minding what you say because of the children'.

In fact, I don't think she even thought of us as children. We were friends, pure and simple, who saw her warts and all. Sometimes we'd bring her home from the bar of the Black Lion Hotel, too drunk to stand up straight and she didn't care who saw it. And sometimes we'd nick her cigars from their supposed hiding place on the bookshelf behind *My People* by Caradoc Evans. She must have known what we were doing, but she never said a word.

She took us poaching salmon with her too, sneaking out at night when no one was about. And she drove without a seat belt because she 'couldna bear to be told what to do'. And it was nothing to find her in the garden on a hot summer's day, not a stitch of clothing on, enjoying the sun and 'damn the melanoma!'

Grace's life was lived in a state of perpetual defiance. I don't think anything she did ever shocked us. If any of our Fitztalbot relatives had done the half of it, they'd have been carted off to the loony bin, but Grace had a way of getting away with things.

She also had a way with words, and an imagination that was second to none. I remember nights under the stars with her – Cary and me huddled in sleeping bags while Grace told tall tales that she insisted were true. We'd look up towards Plynlimon, wondering if it really was a magic mountain like she said, full of secrets and strange powers. There were fairy folk in Grace's tales, elven princes, angels and witches, devils to beware of and shape-shifting wizards whose faces changed from one day to the next.

We knew every story by heart – but the only one she never told us was the one about our father. We knew he'd died in an accident, but had no idea what sort of man he'd been, or what our lives were like before he died, or why our mother never mentioned him. Even

Cary couldn't remember him, though she was older than me. It was as if she'd wiped him from her memory. She certainly never asked anything.

But I did. 'Do I look like him?' I'd ask. 'Do I act like him? Did he love me? Did he hold me as a baby? Why won't our mother talk about him? Did he break her heart?'

Perhaps the questions were the wrong ones – I don't know. But I never got any answers that made sense. Sometimes, playing in St Curig's churchyard, I'd think about his bones and wonder where they lay. Once I remember searching for his grave in the long grass, knowing that it had to be there somewhere. But I couldn't find it, and neither could Grace when I frog-marched her out to look for it.

'It's all so overgrown these days,' she said. 'Don't worry, though – if we can't find it now we'll do it another day.'

We never had done though, but now I had all the time in the world. I opened the gate and started up the path. Maybe my Fitztalbot father had brought me here to banish me, but what I felt was relief. I passed the FOR SALE sign, the builder's board and the concrete mixer, and reached the porch, my heart bursting with an indescribable sense of excitement. It was almost as if, instead of being punished, I'd been set free.

I stamped down the snow and forced open the front door. Inside everything had changed, but I couldn't have cared less. I was just relieved to be back. All Grace's furniture had gone, and so had the carpets on the floors. Walls had come down and rooms been knocked into each other. New floorboards had been laid and white paint slapped over everything.

I walked through the whole house, room after room. In the kitchen, the slate floor had been replaced with ceramic tiles that would have looked all right in sunny Tuscany, but were completely out of place here in Prospect House. Even so, I didn't care. I walked round the whole kitchen with its brand new appliances, knowing that Grace would have hated it, but all I could think was, I'm home. I'm back. It's all right. *I'm safe.*

Safe, but freezing cold. All the old fireplaces had been yanked out and replaced with radiators, and I couldn't find the boiler, or work out how to switch them on. I couldn't even work out how to switch on the lights, and in the end I gave up trying and went to bed.

It was only early, but how else was I going to get warm? I shut my bedroom door, flung myself on to the bed – thanking God that it hadn't been removed, like so much else – wrapped my old quilt round me and tried determinedly not to think.

But this proved impossible. A jumble of images ran through my head, always starting and ending with Cary. And then I didn't feel so carefree. For Cary was my flesh and blood – she was my family, and there was no way I could stay here pretending that everything was all right when I knew it wasn't. Just because my father had banished me, that didn't give me an excuse. I'd put my sister in the hospital, and it was my duty to return to her.

'Tomorrow morning,' I promised myself. 'There's nothing I can do now, but I'll figure out some way of getting back to her first thing.'

I tried to get to sleep, but the morning was hours away and anything could happen between now and then. I lay in bed, listening to a blizzard building up outside the window. Wind gusted down the valley, howling like the *Cŵn y Wbir*, and snow beat against the glass, piling up until I couldn't see outside.

The night felt neverending. I tried to comfort myself by picturing Cary here with me, just like the old days – picturing her being well again and it being summer, with a harvest moon outside the window, fox cubs playing in the newly cut meadow, and voices drifting down from the Black Lion Hotel – songs sung of fairy circles and old hymns of the bread of heaven.

It was a comforting picture and finally it lulled me off to sleep. But in the morning it was still winter, and I was still alone. The view from my bedroom window was hidden by snow, and there was nothing to be heard outside but an echoing silence. I forced the window open and the view that greeted me was of a strange new world that I didn't even know. It was as if the valley had blown away in the night and a new one had come in its place.

I stared across it, trying to pick out landmarks – trees and walls and cottages that might give the landscape its recognisable shape. The Afon Gwy still glinted on its way down the valley, and St Curig's church tower was its usual solid self, rising up behind the trees in Grace's garden. But almost everything else I knew had disappeared. Half the trees had gone, and so had half the houses, hidden by snowdrifts.

Even the huge old yew that marked the boundary of Grace's garden had almost disappeared, hidden by a camouflage of snow. The churchyard behind it was one single carpet, all the gravestones buried. The meadow was a single carpet too, sparkling all the way down to the river. The fields beyond the river were sparkling, and the hills were sparkling too, folding in on each other all the way up the pass road.

I looked at it all, and knew that there was no way I'd get back to Cary today. Nothing I did would get me out of here. Suddenly I felt afraid. I looked at the snow, and it seemed to me that it was winking like thousands of lights, right across the valley. Thousands of corph candles, burning for a death!

What had happened in the night, while I was asleep? Was Cary all right? Had something terrible happened to her? I slammed the window shut and fled the room in search of a phone. But no sooner had I reached the stairs than I caught a glimpse of a light down in the hall. I couldn't hear a sound, but I knew I wasn't imagining it. Somebody was down there – *and they were coming my way!*

I tore back into my bedroom, shut the door, pushed the bed in front of it and dived underneath, pulling the quilt over my head as if the black corph candle was in the house and I had just seen it. I knew that I was being crazy, because it wasn't real, just something out of legend, but I actually felt as if it was coming to get me. The light grew under the door, and then I heard something as well. It sounded like paws padding on bare boards, and there was a snuffling noise too. It came along the landing, heading my way, and I drew back under the bed as far as I could get.

Then I heard a panting noise outside the door and suddenly it wasn't just corph candles that I had to worry about. It was the *Cŵn y Wbir* as well. The dreaded hounds of hell.

No! I thought. *It can't be!* But it seemed it could. Slowly the door began to open, forcing the bed back against the wall, taking me with it. Then the room filled up with light and great grey shapes entered the room, their paws clacking towards me as if they could smell my fear.

They knew exactly where to look for it. I went to pull the quilt over me but, before I could, they looked under the bed and our eyes met. Then a single light started coming towards me and a voice said, 'What are you ... doing down there ... are you all ... right are you ... lost is something ... wrong is that ... really you Zed ... *is it you?*'

Had I been in less of a panic, I would have recognised that voice immediately. Only one person I knew had that broken way of speaking, cutting up his sentences into groups of three words at a time, interrupted by stops.

But, by then, I was past recognising anything. I pulled the quilt right over my head, and it was only when a hand reached under the bed and pulled it off that I finally understood what was going on. A big face, framed by a squashy felt hat, loomed into view.

'It's *you* ...' I said, staring at my father's younger brother – *Pawl Pork-pie.*

7

PAWL PORK-PIE

My mother never had much time for Pawl. I asked her once if he and my father had been alike, and I'll never forget the expression on her face, as if the idea was unthinkable.

Apparently not, I thought, and never dared to ask again.

I suppose he was an embarrassment to her – a big shambling man who couldn't string his words together, tended to wear his clothes back to front and inside out, and often didn't brush or wash his hair because he said it hurt his head. My mother was immaculate, and Pawl was a mess. She was sharp. He was slow. Her life was a matter of achievement, but his was a matter of simply being.

He was confused, and there was nothing he could do about it. He couldn't have told you which year it was, couldn't recite the days of the week, and sometimes couldn't even say what he'd done earlier in the day. How he'd got that way, I'd no idea. Perhaps he'd been born like that, or he'd had an accident or some terrible medical condition like a blood clot on the brain.

I hardly ever thought about it. Pawl was Pawl, and that's all there was to it, as far as I was concerned. I was sorry that my mother never invited him to Pengwern, but I didn't lose much sleep about it because I knew he'd never have fitted in.

Once I remember my mother and Grace having a terse conversation about what would become of Pawl when Grace died. It wasn't that he was unable to look after himself, Grace had said, because he'd made himself a life. And he'd have the money that she left for him, of course, after the house was sold. But what really bothered her was the thought of him being left with nobody to call his own.

'I'm talking about *family*,' Grace had said, looking pointedly at my mother. 'About a sense of *belonging*. I'm talking about giving Pawl *time*. That's what he needs.'

But, if this was a hint, my mother didn't take it. 'Pawl will be just fine,' she said to us afterwards. 'I mean, look at him. It's not as if he's lonely. He likes living on his own. Besides, he's got the whole village for his family. Everybody looks out for him.'

This was true. Everybody was Pawl's friend, from Beryl Breadloaf at the shop to Old Pryce at the Black Lion Hotel. He cut the grass down at the school, and knew every child by name, turning up all year round for non-existent harvest festivals and Christmas carol services, always bringing gifts with him.

Everybody loved Pawl, but nobody did as much as Grace, and now that she was gone he must be missing her dreadfully. Once not a day had passed without him calling in to help out with her gardening or do her odd jobs. In fact, I'd often wondered why he didn't just move in.

But even after Grace had gone, Pawl stayed where he was in his place down by the river, known to everybody as 'the tin house'. He didn't want to live in Prospect House, he said. He was happy with what he'd got. When it came to disposing of Grace's possessions, all that he could be persuaded to take were his mother's fishing rod, her high-backed red wicker sled and her dogs.

It was those dogs that I was looking at now. Not the *Cŵn y Wbir* after all, but not exactly ordinary dogs either! Harri and Mari were the two strangest-looking creatures you could ever wish to see, born of some nameless mix of mongrels that had been in the family for generations. They were huge – as big as calves, Grace always used to say – and they had the wildest, shaggiest grey-brown coats that you ever saw, and eyes that seemed to say things when you looked at them.

I'd known them all my life, and now I climbed out from under the bed, feeling pretty stupid, put my arms around them and greeted them like my long-lost brother and sister. In return they lay their huge paws on my shoulders and almost knocked me flat while Pawl stood watching, a smile on his face. I pulled myself away from them, and greeted him as well.

'Good to see you,' I said, beaming at him, weak with relief.

He beamed back. 'Good to see ... you good to ... have you here ... again it's like ... the old days ... don't like change ... I like things ... better when they

… stay the same.'

This was a big speech for Pawl, who was a private man and didn't give much away about his feelings. At Grace's funeral he hadn't shed a tear. The packed church had wept openly, but Pawl had sat upright, his face stiff beneath his pork-pie hat, his eyes completely dry.

Even when our mother came down afterwards to sort out Prospect House, prior to the builders moving in, Pawl didn't cry. And he certainly wasn't crying now, but I wondered how often he let himself in like this, and wandered round the empty rooms in the early-morning light, telling himself that he liked things better when they stayed the same.

I gave him a hug, and said I agreed. I wouldn't have hugged my Fitztalbot uncles or aunts, and I certainly wouldn't have hugged my father, but Pawl belonged to the old days when Grace had been my family and he had been a part of it. We went downstairs together, and he sorted out the electricity and heating by a mere flick of a switch, then went back to the tin house to fetch me some provisions.

While he was away I looked for the phone, wanting to find out what was happening at the hospital. But I couldn't see it anywhere, and Pawl didn't seem to know where it was either, when he came back. I helped him unload the red wicker sled, which was weighed down with what looked like half his belongings. While I was upstairs making up a proper bed with a duvet, bed linen and pillows, Pawl cooked us both breakfast, his hat still on his head, a bin bag for an apron round his waist and an expression of pure contentment on his face.

He sang as he cooked. You could hear him all over the house. I wished that I could be more like him – could take life as it came instead of always getting in such a state.

'Once I get back to Pengwern,' I promised myself, 'I'm going to turn over a new leaf. I'm going to be nicer to everybody, especially my parents. I'm going to get a grip, and I'm going to work harder. I'll straighten up in school, pass my exams and prove to the Fitztalbot family that Cary's not the only one who's got a brain.'

Pawl called out that breakfast was ready. I hurried downstairs, and he might have trouble with his words, but it was obvious that Pawl could cook. I sat down before the perfect breakfast, especially for a boy who'd eaten almost nothing for the last two days. Bacon that was thick and crisp; sausages that were juicy without being fatty; scrambled eggs that were as light and soft as summer sunshine; toast that was as crumbly as if the bread had only just been baked; butter that tasted like home-whipped cream, and jam that smelt of early-morning dew in Grace's strawberry patch.

I ate it all, washed down with coffee that achieved the impossible and actually tasted as good as it smelt. The whole thing was astonishing. In all the years I'd been coming down to Wales, I'd never seen this side of Pawl before. You think you know people, but you don't.

He ate his breakfast too, beaming with pleasure as I heaped praise upon him. In between mouthfuls, he tried to tell me all the local gossip. But I couldn't understand the half of it and, besides, the combination of food and warmth was finally getting to me.

My eyelids drooped and, in the end, I had to make my excuses and go up to bed. The house was warm now, and I was comfortable. Finally the trauma of the last few days was catching up with me. I closed my eyes and fell fast asleep.

When I awoke, it was getting dark. I could smell more cooking coming from the kitchen, and went downstairs to discover that, flushed with his success, Pawl had gone berserk. Covering every available work-surface were racks of biscuits, sponge cakes, muffins, sausage rolls and mince pies. Some of them were burned, but some of them were fine. In the oven was a loaf of bread, and on the brand new hob sat a hotpot of what my grandmother always used to call 'sweet mountain lamb'. Dishes were piled in the sink, and the dishwasher was full.

The fridge was full as well, and so were all the cupboards. You'd have thought that I had come to stay for months. I swallowed hard. I'd never seen Pawl looking so pleased with himself. I wondered how I was ever going to explain to him about my need to return to Pengwern.

Before I could explain anything, however, he took me by the arm and steered me down the hall to Grace's parlour at the back of the house, telling me that I should go and sit with her and keep her company.

'She waits for ... you I'll bring ... you in some ... tea and cakes,' he said.

His words went through me. Surely Pawl knew that Grace was dead? I wasn't going to have to explain it to him, was I? Besides, the last thing I wanted was to enter Grace's parlour and see it empty. It had always been her nest, full of bits and pieces that she'd gathered and brought home, knitting them together into a perfect whole. I hadn't been able to face it after the funeral, and I hadn't been able to face it later, when my mother went to sort it out.

She'd gone sweeping in with determination, saying it was a dirty job but 'had to be done'. Clouds of dust had been raised and boxes had been dispatched to the garage to either 'deal with later' or give away. But I had refused to touch a thing. I wouldn't even enter the room.

And I wouldn't have entered it now if Pawl hadn't given me a push and sent me flying in – only to discover that everything was back in its place. I stared at Grace's books and magazines, her paintings, her pens, notebooks, fossils, feathers, stuffed fish, old glass jars and jumble of everything from knitting needles to seed trays. It was as if she'd never gone away. I could smell her whisky, and even a whiff of her secret hoard of cigars. I went to look behind the Caradoc Evans on the bookshelf, and there they were, back where she had always kept them. Everything was in its place. Everything was back.

Even the dust was back.

I tried to speak, but couldn't manage a single word. Pawl brought in the promised tea and cakes and set them down. He was grinning with pride – a happy, grown-up child who seemed to think that he had cheated death. I remembered what he'd said about not liking change. It must have taken him months to get the room back to how it had been in the old days. But he'd worked away at it until he'd got everything exactly right.

'Sit with Grace,' he said.

I looked at Grace's chair, and understood. It was almost as if she was in the room with us. I'd thought she'd gone for ever, but now I could almost feel her presence again.

Pawl lit the fire, then flung himself down in a chair and closed his eyes. I knew he wasn't asleep, but savouring his achievement. I sat opposite him, and a companionable silence fell between us. Firelight danced on the walls and the day outside grew slowly darker. Harri and Mari lay at our feet, basking in front of the fire. There was something peaceful about them, and about the strange half-light. I could have stayed like that for hours, listening to them sighing in their sleep and watching Pawl smiling with his eyes shut.

But then the phone started ringing – the phone I'd tried so hard to find earlier, but now here it was when I least wanted it. I knew who would be ringing, but didn't want to answer. It rang on and on, and in the end Pawl went and got it.

'Hello this is ... Pawl that's right ... Happy Christmas to ... you it's snowy ... here how's Pengwern ... Zed's here shall ... I call him?' he said.

Or something like that, anyway.

I got to my feet, braced to face my mother. Down the hall, Pawl was nodding and frowning, and I could hear my mother's voice buzzing down the line. But Pawl didn't call me over and finally, after a simple unadorned 'yes', followed by an equally stark 'no', there was a loud click and Pawl was left holding a humming receiver.

He stared at it, as if he didn't quite know what had happened. 'What did she say to you?' I asked.

'A happy Christmas ...' Pawl said, shaking his head. 'She wishes us ... a happy Christmas ... '

I walked away. I knew that there was more to it than that, but Pawl obviously couldn't get the words out. The day was spoiled, and suddenly I wanted to be alone. I went up to my room and sat in the dark, looking out of the window and thinking how much my mother must hate me, to not even want to speak to me.

But who could blame her, after what I'd done?

Outside the wind got up again, blowing down the valley and bringing with it a fresh fall of snow. Grace always said that Prospect House had the best views in the village, but that it paid for them by taking the brunt of the bad weather. It was doing that now, the walls buffeted by the wind, and the windowpanes thick with running streams of flakes.

Downstairs, the front door closed and Pawl slipped away as if the special moment was over and he'd got things to be getting on with – either that or else he'd heard the bad news about Cary and wanted to nurse his feelings on his own. I heard the sled skimming over the snow and the dogs running with it. Then the sound was gone, and all I could hear was the wind.

I leant against the window. It was pitch dark out there in the night, and I felt like the sole survivor in a crumbling world. I searched for signs of life and it was then, underneath the old yew tree that marked Grace's boundary, that I saw the candle. It was burning without flickering despite the storm raging around it. I wasn't imagining it. I really saw it.

A black corph candle, *burning for a death*.

8

ON PLYNLIMON

That night I hung a blanket over the window to make sure that I didn't see anything else. I was terrified of what the candle meant, and why it had come to me. I called home but there was no reply, called the hospital, but the only news that the nurse would give out over the phone was that my sister was 'stable', whatever that meant.

I hardly slept that night. I didn't for a minute believe that 'stable' was anything to feel at peace about. Every time I dropped off, I dreamt of Cary lying in her hospital bed surrounded by machines. Morning came as a relief. I had fallen asleep around dawn, and now awoke late to the sound of bells.

I removed the blanket from the window with some trepidation, only to find a bright day outside. The landscape was as white as ever, but the snow clouds had blown away and people were out and about. It was like coming into shore from a distant sea voyage. Children played in the snow down the meadow by the river, and the ringing sound of shovels clearing paths could be heard across the village.

Suddenly I was back in the real world again, with my feet firmly on the ground. It wasn't something out of legend that was going on outside my window, but real life. I watched people struggling up the church path, answering the call of St Curig's Sunday morning bell. I knew each and every one of them, knew their names and who they were related to and who was friends with whom.

The last to come was Pawl, gliding down the path in Grace's red wicker sled. He disappeared into the shadow of the church porch, pausing only to take off his pork-pie hat and stuff it into his coat pocket. Then the bells stopped ringing and the organ started playing carols.

For the first time in days, I felt as if Christmas was on the way. It was a beautiful morning. The storm had gone. The sky was bright. The valley glittered like a jewel and I had my first clear view of Plynlimon. Its flanks glistened, white upon white, whilst the Afon Gwy twisted down from it like a silver corkscrew.

It was a perfect picture-postcard view. I sat and watched the river flowing past the village. Back in Pengwern, people thought the queen of rivers was their Sabrina Fludde, but I knew that the Afon Gwy was the only queen. Suddenly I found myself pleading with it to save my sister's life. Pleading as if it was a real queen, and had the power to grant requests.

'I don't care what becomes of me,' I pleaded. 'Don't care if my family never speaks to me again. All I care about is Cary. Please, oh please, *let my sister live*!'

The Afon Gwy didn't answer. It just flowed on down the valley, giving no sign of having heard.

Feeling a fool for expecting anything else, I got dressed and went downstairs to call home. I couldn't get through, yet again, but discovered that, sometime in the night, my mother had left a message on the answerphone.

'There's nothing to report,' she said. 'The ward sister told us that you'd phoned, but it's probably better if *we* call you rather than *you* call us. If there's any change we'll let you know.'

I played the message through a couple of times, wanting to hear her voice again, even though I knew she must have phoned in the night to avoid hearing mine. Over in the church, the organ had stopped playing and I could hear the mumble of chanted prayers. Suddenly I wanted to pray too. I don't know what made me think of it, but I wanted to sit in the pews with everybody else, and feel like I belonged, and pray for Cary in the hope that God would hear me better than the river had done.

I hurried out of the house, pulling on my coat, staggered down the garden and over the churchyard wall, and headed for the church. I should have just marched in, but I stopped in the porch, waiting for the right moment. My eyes ran down the rotas on the church noticeboard – the lists of committees for famine relief, missionary work in South America, luncheon clubs, volunteer car-share schemes, baby-sitting circles, flower arranging clubs and a string of other worthy activities.

By the time I reached the end of them, I knew I couldn't possibly enter the church. What place was there for me amongst these worthy people and their good deeds? A boy like me, whose sister's life hung in the balance because of what he'd done? What would these people on the rotas make of me, if they only knew? They'd wash their hands of me, just like my parents had done. Even Pawl would wash his hands of me. Even him!

Inside the church, the chanting ended and another carol started up. I crept away, knowing that I couldn't join in. The sun was still shining in a sky still dazzling blue, but it didn't feel like a beautiful morning any more. A chasm had opened up between myself and everybody else. I'd thought I had come home, but I'd got it wrong. Because of what I'd done, I *had* no home.

At the church lych-gate, I broke into a trot. I had no idea where I would end up, but couldn't get out of the village quickly enough. I started up the Plynlimon pass road, trying to put as much distance as possible between myself and the sound of good Welsh hymn singing. It was a stupid thing to do – not least because I wasn't dressed for going anywhere. My coat was thin. My trainers were useless in the snow. I didn't have a hat or scarf or even any gloves.

But nothing could have persuaded me to turn back. I passed the cottages above the Bluebell Inn, and the village fell behind me. The last cottage disappeared from sight, hidden by a sweep of trees, and the mountain stood ahead. I knew that it was treacherous, even at the best of times. People went up there and never came back – I knew that as well as anyone.

But I ploughed on all the same, following what I thought was the road, until it dawned on me that I was lost. I couldn't possibly be on the pass road, I decided, but was on one of the mountain tracks that cut up between Forestry Commission land. By now, the shape of the valley had changed drastically and I couldn't pick out a single landmark. What should I do? I asked myself. Press on through the snow, hoping to reach the next village over the mountain? Look for a barn to shelter in? Turn round, and try to find my way back?

I cursed myself for my stupidity. What had I been playing at? Plynlimon was no mountain to mess around on. It was completely unpredictable, as anybody with sense knew. The sun could shine on it one minute, and it could be shrouded in the deepest and most treacherous mist the next.

In the end, unable to decide what else to do, I carried on. Trees surrounded me until I couldn't see the valley any more. Fingers of mist started weaving their way towards me, and I was beginning to panic when I suddenly saw a gate with a house set back behind it.

It was a long, low, half-timbered house that had obviously seen happier days. Some of its windowpanes were broken, and I couldn't see a light in any of them. But I *could* see smoke rising from a single, tall chimney pot. The smoke of hearth and home – or so I hoped.

I hauled myself over the gate, and made my way towards the house, trudging up a snowy drive. As I drew level with the stable block I saw a couple of abandoned cars and a battered-looking old bus decorated with the slogans '*WONDER OF ALL WONDERS*' and '*THE AMAZING DR KATTERFELTO*'.

As soon as I saw the words, I realised where I was. I

didn't know 'the amazing Dr Katterfelto' personally but, like everybody else, I knew that he lived at Clockvine House, halfway up Plynlimon Mountain. Down in the village he was the source of endless speculation. He was a Doctor of Conjuring, internationally famous, living with his daughter, Gilda, who worked as his assistant.

The village was full of gossip about them both, but nobody knew anything for a fact. Sometimes you'd catch a glimpse of light between the trees of Clockvine Wood, but, for months at a time, they would be dark because the Katterfeltos were away on tour in their battered old bus.

I only saw it once, but it stuck in my memory because it happened just before Grace died. We'd been returning home from the Black Lion Hotel, and the bus came tearing past us, driven by Dr Katterfelto in his black four-cornered conjuror's hat and cloak, Gilda by his side, wearing a green silk costume.

The moon had caught them both as they shot past – caught their eyes and made them glint like silver. Then they'd been gone, carrying on up the pass road, leaving a distinct impression of something strange having passed our way.

The word about the village – depending on whether you drank in the Bluebell Inn or the Black Lion Hotel – was that the Katterfeltos were either eccentric millionaires who conjured for a hobby, or were living in destitution without even electricity. Either showmen or reclusives, father and daughter or lovers, Prussian aristocracy or as Welsh as anybody else, having taken on a fancy stage name in their desire to impress.

And now I had the chance to find out for myself! I

hammered on the front door, knowing that I was done for if I couldn't make them hear.

Please God, I thought, raising the knocker. Please let them answer. Please may they be in. Please, oh please!

A cat miaowed inside the house, but that was all. I knocked again, and then again, and was about to give up and go round the back when a voice came towards me from what felt like a great distance.

'*All right, all right!*' it called. 'I'm coming. Don't be so impatient.'

I heard footsteps behind the door, and suddenly it flew open to reveal a man with sandy-coloured hair, a holey sweater with dandruff on its shoulders, baggy trousers and Winnie the Pooh slippers. We stared at each other. It was hard to recognise him as Dr Katterfelto, but that was who he was. I tried to speak, but didn't need to.

'Good grief!' the man said, in a voice that could have been Prussian, like some people said, or it could have been Welsh – or anything else. 'Look at the state of you! What are you doing out there on my drive? Don't just stand there like that, boy – come inside, or you'll freeze to death!'

9

HOCUS POCUS

My first thought, upon entering Clockvine House, was that I'd made a terrible mistake. I might have been freezing cold and half dead, but it had always been drummed into me that I should never go anywhere with people I didn't know. Not only that, but the inside of the house was almost as dark and inhospitable as the mountain upon which it had been built. By the time I'd got to the end of the long hall, I could hardly see my way back to the front door.

I began to feel sick and slightly panicky. The place had a musty, cold smell about it, and I was just beginning to think that the local gossipmongers had been right about it lacking electricity, when a door opened and a voice said, 'Really, Pa. What are you doing, stumbling around in the dark? You'll trip over the carpet if you're not careful.'

A light went on, and there stood Gilda Katterfelto. Her eyes were like bright emeralds and her hair was dark. Her father explained about finding me on the doorstep and sent her upstairs to fetch warm clothes. I changed straight into them, a baggy sweater, jogging bottoms, slippers and thick socks, then allowed myself to be led into their sitting room, where a fire was burning.

'Sit down,' Dr Katterfelto said. 'What's your name? Zed? Well, Zed, pull up a chair and get warmed up.'

I did as I was bidden, and immediately began to feel better. The Katterfeltos might be strangers, but they couldn't be kinder. Gilda disappeared into the kitchen and returned with a trolley laden with tea and a cake. It was as if I was an honoured guest. Her father poured the tea while she sliced the cake with a silver knife.

'I hope you're hungry,' she said. 'Help yourself.'

I didn't need to be asked twice. Suddenly my being here didn't feel like a mistake. I piled my plate high, then emptied it, then did the same again, and then again. Before too long my life began to take on a distinct glow. Gilda sat at my elbow, wielding the cake knife, while Dr Katterfelto topped me up with tea and filled my awkward silences with tales about his show-business life.

He was a brilliant storyteller, full of tales he couldn't possibly have made up because, on every wall, I could see the photographs that proved him right. I looked at a pop legend from the sixties, proud to shake the doctor's hand. A famous violinist. A late-night newsreader. A politician. Even a minor royal.

'Before you ask,' said Dr Katterfelto, following my eyes, 'I've met them all. Kings and princes, lords and ladies – you name them and I've performed for them. I've put on shows in palaces, and I've put them on in village halls. High and low – it makes no difference.

And I'll put on one for you. Test-drive my latest tricks on you – if you'd like me to, that is.'

My plate was empty by this time, and so was my cup. Gilda nodded at the cake, but I shook my head. She wheeled the trolley out of the way, and I said that I would love to see the doctor's new tricks. At this, he rose to his feet.

'Shall we go, then?' he said.

I was more than willing. The three of us set off through the house, down yet more long, dark corridors, through a pair of glazed double doors, and into an elegant old conservatory. Its great expanse of glass revealed a sky full of stars, and I realised for the first time that night had fallen. Dr Katterfelto pulled up a cane chair between a pair of potted palms, and told me to make myself comfortable. Then he and Gilda made their way down the conservatory to a makeshift stage full of props.

'Just give us a minute while we put on our costumes,' he called, as he climbed on to the stage.

Gilda climbed up after him. As she picked her way between their props, she pulled on her green silk costume and matching cap, tucking her hair up into it. The doctor started getting dressed up too, pulling on white gloves, a black cloak and a black, four-cornered hat until, finally, he stood centre-stage, utterly transformed.

It was as if a piece of magic had already taken place. Gilda was transformed as well. She didn't look like a young girl any more, but a woman of dark mystery. And Dr Katterfelto didn't look shabby. There wasn't even a hint of dandruff on his shoulders and he definitely didn't look like the sort of man who'd wear

Winnie the Pooh slippers. Instead he stood tall – a Doctor of Conjuring, and the undisputed master of Clockvine House conservatory, not to say anything of village halls and palaces!

I found myself clapping. He hadn't done a trick yet, and I was already impressed. Gilda smiled and bowed, turning towards her father who cried out in a whole, new, ringing voice: 'Wonders! Wonders! Wonders! I will show you wonders! Greater wonders, my friend Zed, than you will ever see in your whole life!'

And I believed him. How could I not? The show hadn't even begun, and already I was on the edge of my seat! Dr Katterfelto threw back his cloak and, in his hands, he held a long golden hunting horn. He raised it to his lips and blew, and immediately the tall palms on either side of me started rustling like trees in a forest when a storm's on the way.

'Let the wonders commence!' Dr Katterfelto cried, and suddenly the air was alive with circles of light. They looked like silver moons between the palms. I watched them rise up the conservatory, casting shadows outside in the snowy garden. One by one, they reached the top of the glass and started fluttering down again like white-frocked ballerinas doing pirouettes.

I stared at them in astonishment. I didn't know where they'd come from, nor what had brought them into being. All I knew was that they were beautiful. As I watched, they formed themselves into an arc over the stage. Then patterns appeared on each of them, moving and shuffling across their surfaces like the shapes in a kaleidoscope. One circle filled with dancing snowflakes. Another filled with dark, winged birds. Another filled with floating clouds. Another filled with flowers opening out into exotic shapes.

Then Dr Katterfelto clapped his hands, and the circles disappeared like lights going out. But the moving shapes remained. Not only that, but they came to life! Suddenly clouds were drifting between the palms, and flowers bursting out all around the conservatory. Snow was falling on my face, and birds were flying everywhere. I felt their wings stir the air above my head. For a moment, they were *that* real. And then they disappeared as well, and the conservatory was plunged into darkness.

I clapped until my hands stung. 'You think *that* was a wonder?' Dr Katterfelto cried out, taking centre stage again. 'Well, what do you think of *this*?'

He threw back his black conjuror's cloak. Gilda came and stood in front of him, pressed her cheek against his chest and stood perfectly still while he wrapped his cloak around her until all that could be seen were her head and feet. Then Dr Katterfelto cried out, 'Wonders! Wonders! Wonders!' and, at the first 'Wonder', Gilda's feet disappeared, at the second, her head disappeared, and at the third, the rest of her went too.

Dr Katterfelto threw back his cloak and Gilda had gone. All that remained – tucked into the crook of his arm – was a small, black cat with emerald eyes. Dr Katterfelto lifted it up, and I clapped and clapped. I didn't really believe that the doctor had turned Gilda into a cat, but, before I could work out what else he'd done with her, he started on his next trick.

It was even better than the last. Dr Katterfelto ran his hand down the cat and its body started slowly vanishing. It happened right before my eyes – no cloak to hide behind this time, no mirrors, tricks or sleight-of-hand that I could see. Finally everything vanished, except for the cat's tail that hung, disembodied, in the air. Then Dr Katterfelto ran a single, white-gloved finger down the tail and – with a little fizz of blue light – that vanished too!

I stared in unbelief, too astonished even to clap. But Dr Katterfelto hadn't finished with me yet. From his pocket he produced a small biscuit wrapped in tissue paper. He unwrapped the biscuit, which he gave to me, but retained its paper, which he lit with a match and then let go. It rose to the top of the conservatory, burning all the way like a bright star, then slowly fell back down again until Dr Katterfelto caught it in his cupped hands.

By this time, it was nothing but a skeletal piece of grey ash. Dr Katterfelto held it up for me to see, and there in his palm – I swear this, honestly – was a miniature Gilda! A tiny model of her, perfect in every detail, except that it was made of ash. And then the doctor clapped his hands and the ash turned into a poof of smoke – *and Gilda was back!*

For a moment she stood against her father, her cheek pressed against his chest. Then she burst out laughing, and I found myself laughing too, and clapping as if I'd never stop. Dr Katterfelto bowed, and Gilda bowed as well, turning to her father as if he was the undisputed master.

Then Dr Katterfelto said, 'That's enough for one day. I think it's time to take you home.'

I didn't want to go home, but didn't have much choice. Dr Katterfelto brought his tour bus round to the front of the house and we climbed in. I imagined flying down the valley fuelled by nothing more than hocus pocus, but by now Dr Katterfelto had removed his conjuror's costume and got back into his holey old sweater. He had returned to ordinary life, and so had I.

Gilda tied the bus door shut with a piece of string, and I sat on the front seat next to her, staring out of the window. The house fell away from us with a final glimpse of the conservatory. Then it was gone and we were hurtling down the mountain, cutting through banks of snow and careering over ice.

Dr Katterfelto was a real devil of a driver. Every time we took a bank or bend too fast, he cursed in an accent that was far from Prussian. Several times I had to grab the seat, and hold on tight to stop myself from being thrown about. But he called out that I mustn't worry – he'd done more journeys in this broken-down old bus than I'd eaten hot dinners, and he knew what he was doing.

This was hardly reassuring, given the speed at which we were travelling and the condition of the bus. But finally the village came into view – the village and my old life again, waiting for me like an answerphone full of nasty messages. The closer it got, the more my heart sank. For a few strange, happy hours, I had forgotten who I was, and why I'd run away, and what I'd done to Cary. But now I remembered everything.

All too soon, we pulled up outside Prospect House. I wished I could turn back the clock and find myself in the conservatory again, clapping wildly. 'Thanks for everything,' I said, climbing down from the bus and standing shivering on the lane. 'I really mean it. The tea, and the lift, and the show especially.'

'Get yourself inside,' said Dr Katterfelto. 'Make yourself a hot drink. Get an early night, and make sure you put an extra blanket on your bed – it's going to get even colder tonight.'

He smiled, and so did Gilda. I stood and watched as the bus turned round in the road. Then they were gone, disappearing into the darkness like a conjuror's trick, their two faces turned away as if they'd forgotten me already.

10

THE BLACK CANDLE

When I got indoors, there was a new message from my mother on the answerphone. In a voice I hardly recognised, it announced that Cary had slipped deeper into her coma and that it was unreasonable, in the words of the hospital, 'to offer too much hope at this stage'.

'It's best that you still stay where you are,' my mother said, every word clipped and tight. 'Cary wouldn't know that you were here, and we couldn't possibly come and get you, anyway.'

I went to Grace's parlour, glad that I'd been out when the call came through, and that I hadn't been required to answer it personally. In the dresser I found Grace's whisky and, behind the Caradoc Evans, I found her cigars. I helped myself to both and sat nursing them before the ashes of the previous night's fire. I couldn't feel Grace's presence any more. This was just an empty room, its owner gone away never to return. And my sister wouldn't return either. She, too, was slipping away.

I was on my second tot of whisky, and had puffed enough of a cigar to make myself feel sick when Pawl came in. I didn't hear him until too late, but there he suddenly was, standing in the doorway, seemingly unaware of my guilty attempts to hide what I'd been up to.

'Came down earlier ... Welsh lamb stew ... heated up lunch ... you all right ... couldn't find you ...' he said.

Now he'd brought me supper instead and, no matter how sick from smoking I felt, I knew I couldn't turn it down. Pawl was in a funny mood. He sat down opposite me, but didn't smile. I pushed my supper around my plate, and he didn't exactly watch me but then he didn't exactly look away. It was as if something was bothering him, but he couldn't bring himself to say it.

Everything felt changed since yesterday. Even the room felt changed. Pawl didn't light the fire, and didn't lean back and savour things the way he'd done the night before. I wondered if he, too, had had a phone call from my mother, saying that he shouldn't phone her but that she'd phone him. Or perhaps the problem lay elsewhere.

I looked around the parlour, full of Grace's things that she'd never touch again. Yesterday it had seemed alive, buzzing with the very essence of her personality. But now it felt like a museum – Pawl's Gracelife Museum, you could almost say – and I wondered if Pawl was finally realising that she wasn't coming back.

I went and sat on the edge of his chair, and put my arm around his shoulder. Pawl leant against it, as if he was my child. There were secrets in his face – things I couldn't understand and, from the look of him, I guessed he couldn't understand them either. We sat in silence. All sorts of things ran through my mind – a jumble of crazy, upset thoughts, but I couldn't find the words for any of them.

Suddenly Pawl started talking – *about my father*. 'A good old ... boy your father ... was you know ... laughed he did ... always laughed he ... was always full ... of good fun ... tired I am ... of missing him ... you look just ... like his son ... glad he'd be ... to see you ... all grown-up ... his big boy ... and proud too ... he would be ... proud of you ...'

He squeezed my hand. I tried to smile. My father might have been proud of me once, I thought, but not any more – not after what I've done to Cary!

Silence hung between us. Pawl had tried to tell me something that would make me feel better about myself. It was as if he'd sensed that I'd needed it. But it hadn't worked, and he knew it. In the end, he got up, cleared away the supper things and left me on my own, telling me to make sure that all the doors and windows were secured because another bout of storm was on the way.

He was right, too. I didn't quite believe him at the time, because the night was clear and starry, but I awoke in the early hours to find the windowpanes rattling and the whole house groaning. The night was freezing cold as well, and ice had formed on the insides of the windows.

I lay in bed, watching snowflakes dancing outside, filling up the darkness with wild swirling light. The scaffolding on the front of the house was rattling fit to fly away, and gusts of wind had worked their way under the slates, making the roof moan as if it was in agony.

In the morning, I found the phone line down and the electricity off. It was too cold to get out of bed, and I was snowed in again. I knew my parents didn't want me at the hospital, but I also knew I had to get there. I'd thought of little else all night, and got up determined to do the best I could.

I dressed properly for it this time, with double layers of gloves, boots lined with plastic bags as well as socks and a huge old coat along with other clothing that I found in the shed and piled on too. No way was I going to be beaten by the cold again!

When I was ready, I started digging my way out. Quite how I'd make it out of the village, let alone all the way back to Pengwern, I'd no idea. But I'd wasted days already and was determined not to waste any more.

I forced the porch door open and started shovelling my way first up the path, then up the lane. No one else was around yet, and the morning was silent and overcast.

I got up to the main road, where the gritter had been out, and started trudging through the village. What I should have done was knock on some door, any door: Mr Pryce's at the Black Lion Hotel, or anybody else's, and ask for help. But I was too ashamed at the thought of anybody knowing what I'd done to Cary, so I carried on until the village lay behind me and a wilderness lay ahead, seemingly without boundaries. I couldn't even see a hedge or wall to mark the edge of the road. In fact, the gritter had given up and I couldn't even see the road.

All I had to guide me was the Afon Gwy. I followed it as best I could, heading in the direction of what I hoped was the main dual carriageway back to Pengwern. If everything else was snowed in, I reckoned, at least this all-important north–south route would have been cleared.

I walked for ages, but couldn't find my way, and didn't even hear any traffic. It began to snow again – the sort of nasty, wet snow that sticks to everything it touches like iron filings to a magnet. I kept wiping it out of my eyes, but the snowfall just got heavier and finally I could hardly see where I was going. I couldn't find the river any more, and the hills and mountains had completely disappeared, buried in low clouds. I couldn't even see the village behind me.

When I saw a boy, therefore, he came as a relief. He was out in one of the fields, wrapped against the weather in a duffle-coat and red woolly hat, engaged in throwing snowballs at sheep. Where he lived, I'd no idea, because I couldn't see a house, but he stopped what he was doing at the sight of me and had the grace to look guilty.

I pretended I couldn't see the snowball in the hand behind his back. 'I'm looking for the main road,' I called. 'I know it's round here somewhere, but I seem to have lost my sense of direction.'

The boy paused for a moment, as if considering what I'd said, then he pointed to a line of snow-laden trees on the edge of Forestry Commission land. 'That would be your quickest bet,' he called back. 'If you carry on as you are now, it'll take you for ever, but if you cut up through the trees, you'll find the road on the far side. It's quite a climb, but it'll save you time.'

I thanked the boy, and headed where he pointed. He started throwing snow at sheep again, chuckling to himself as if he'd cracked some sort of joke. He turned out to be right, too, about the climb, but I didn't mind. At least I was getting somewhere, I told myself. I was doing something about my sister. I was heading back to her – and I had the strangest feeling that she knew. It was almost as if she was with me already, here in spirit, sharing the journey.

I started singing – crazy, wild songs that I was sure Cary sang with me, the two of us in harmony, despite everything that kept us apart. But after a while, the journey started taking its toll. There seemed no end to the trees; I couldn't shake them off, and couldn't find the top of the hill, let alone the road beyond it.

I began to wonder if the boy had played a trick on me, in just the same spirit that he'd thrown snowballs at sheep. My feet dragged and my hands throbbed despite the double layers of gloves. My ears discovered by experience what the *bite* in 'frostbite' was all about, and the songs froze in my throat.

I don't know what would have happened if I hadn't seen the lights of a cottage. Suddenly I noticed it ahead of me, and saw a garden with a hedge running round it, and heard voices calling to each other. I forced myself forward, all inhibitions lost about asking for help. Perhaps somebody could be persuaded to take me to the main road, or even the next town. Or perhaps they'd even have pity on me, and take me all the way to Pengwern.

You never know, I thought. Grace always said how kind country people could be. She said they were the salt of the earth.

I approached the garden, trying to call for help, but my voice was still frozen in my throat, and I couldn't make a sound. I reached the hedge. I could see the cottage but couldn't get to it. I could also see figures in the garden – a dad and his kids trying to build a snow-castle, complete with towers and battlements.

As I watched, they gave up on their efforts and went indoors, shaking off the snow and laughing to each other as if they didn't know that they'd left someone behind, freezing against their hedge. The last to enter was the dad and, just for a moment, I could have sworn he sensed that something was up. He hesitated in the doorway as if he actually might come back. But then he smiled to himself and shut the door – and I could have wept. I'd never felt so bleak in my whole life. Never such an outsider.

I leant against the hedge, feeling utterly alone. I couldn't even sense my sister's presence any more. It was as if she'd gone, and all my hopes had gone with her.

And that was when I saw the candle.

It was in the distance, between the trees – the same black candle, I could have sworn, that I'd seen the other night. But then I had been terrified, and now I found myself furious. *How dare the candle come and gloat at me?* I looked at it, shining in the darkness but throwing out no light. Suddenly I found myself lunging at it. Half of me wanted to snuff it out, destroying it so that it could never burn again and frighten anybody else. But the other half wanted to take hold of it, as if it was my sister's very life itself, and keep her safe by keeping it alive.

Torn between the two, I staggered through the forest, following the candle, which was always just out of reach, until the trees fell behind me and I found myself on open moorland. Here the snow fell so thickly that I could hardly see my hands in front of my face. The ground beneath my feet looked like a great white bed – one that I would love to lie down and fall asleep in, but I knew I couldn't. If I stopped, I told myself, I'd have had it, and so would Cary.

So I forced myself on, even though I couldn't see the candle any more, or anything else apart from snow. My legs got slower and my body felt increasingly removed from the real me. My eyelids drooped and I could scarcely keep them open. Finally I found myself on hands and knees. I didn't know how I'd got there, but I crawled into the shelter of an upturned tree root and curled up into a tight ball.

I knew that I should carry on looking for the candle, but I couldn't take another step. Couldn't do a thing but give up the fight. I closed my eyes – and there, inside my head, I found the candle waiting for me, burning without flickering, still giving out no light.

11

THE WHITE HOUSE

I awoke to find myself in a white house made of snow. Everything around me shone, and I thought at first that I'd died and gone to heaven. Snow lay across me in a blanket as soft as lamb's wool, and the air around me glittered with tiny crystals.

I lay perfectly still, frozen by the moment like a new-born baby before the first yell. In the walls around me I could see crystallised flowers and leaves, and icicles hung over my head like Christmas tree baubles.

'Is this place *real*?' I asked myself. 'Am I dead? And, if not, *what's happened to me*?'

I got up to investigate. The floor beneath my feet was carpeted with snow and the air was icy cold. But, strangest of all, leaning out of a window, I could see Plynlimon Mountain spread out around me. Instead of being where I'd thought I was, somewhere between the village and the main road back to Pengwern, I was on the open mountain with views that stretched to the horizon.

It was a brand new day and the sun was shining. Yesterday's snowstorm had blown itself out, and I could see hills and silver rivers, ridges of dark forest and villages clustered beneath smoking chimneys. Over it all was spread a bright blue enamelled sky and, on the very edge of the sky – at the point where it joined forces with the land – I could even catch a glimpse of the sea.

It was just a strip of gold, shimmering in the distance like a hot road on a summer's day. But at the sight of it, my heart skipped a beat. I had always loved the sea, and now I could almost smell its salt tang and feel the tidal pull of its horizon, full of promise and adventure. I watched it winking on the edge of my vision, full of life, moving to a rhythm of its own, and I wanted to be there more than anywhere else. Here I was, stuck on Plynlimon by some extraordinary misdirection that I couldn't quite work out. And there it was – the gateway to a land beyond the winter snows.

I turned away, only one thing on my mind – getting back into the world that I could see from the window. But the house was bigger than I'd expected, and I couldn't find the way out. Every staircase led to another, and every corridor did the same. It almost felt like a city, with high roads and low ones, and dead-end back ways, and evidence of life everywhere but not a soul in sight.

I passed through snow-white bedrooms with slippers frozen to the floor and dressing gowns frozen to the backs of doors, high-ceilinged bathrooms full of burst pipes sporting water sculptures frozen into weird shapes, frozen remains of half-eaten meals on plates, and even toothbrushes in bathrooms, sitting in glasses of solid crystal. But I never saw a single person. And, when I called, 'Is anybody there?' I never got any reply.

It was as if the house had been abandoned and the elements had taken over. I ran down corridors that felt like crevasses, getting colder all the time, and narrower as well. This place was impossible to escape. I turned towards its lower regions, but even down there in the basement, I couldn't find a way out.

I stumbled from one room to another, lit only by occasional windows, looking out on patches of darkening sky. 'Is anybody there?' I called again, but I still never got any reply.

In the end, I decided to turn back. I was beginning to get frightened. I'd been here for what like felt like hours, and was no closer to finding the way out. The house wasn't a city, I decided – it was a maze. I felt my way along the wall, and suddenly I heard the bark of dogs in the distance. It was the first sound of life I'd heard all day, and I turned towards it. I hoped to find a yard somewhere with a gate on it, but when I stumbled through a door, pushing it open, it wasn't a yard I found on the other side.

It was another basement room – and no sooner had I entered it than the door closed behind me, seemingly of its own accord! It melted into the wall and I was trapped. In a panic, I flung myself at the walls, trying to find the way out. Then I heard the dogs again, and realised that they were in the room with me, hidden somewhere in its shadows. I spun round, certain that I could hear them breathing. Then I heard something else as well – and I couldn't have said why exactly, but the sense of another person in the room with me was overwhelming.

I wasn't alone, and suddenly I knew it. I peered through the darkness and, for the first time, noticed a pinprick of light. I moved towards it, and a pair of eyes came into view, lit by a stub of candle cupped in a pair of hands.

A stub of black corph candle.

Just for a moment, everything stopped. I couldn't hear a sound, not even the dogs. Then a figure stepped out of the shadows, and I knew who he was. I'd never really believed in him, despite all Grace's stories – but he was real after all.

'*You're the Red Judge of Plynlimon!*' I said.

The man looked down at me, but didn't answer, his eyes as black as curses. My mouth went dry. I was caught, like a fox run to ground. And yet it wasn't fear that gripped me. Instead, it was the strangest sense of opportunity. I looked at the candle. If it burned for me, I reckoned, then it also burned for Cary. The two of us together. That was what I'd felt on my way up the mountain, and now I felt it again. Ever since the accident, I'd longed for a chance to say sorry and put things right. Now here was that chance. It was what I'd set out for, not knowing where I was going. This wasn't a trap after all – *it was my chance to make amends*.

Alarm bells rang inside my head, but I wouldn't heed them. 'You've got to help me,' I begged the red judge. 'You're the one who's got the power. I'd pay any price to save my sister's life. I'm to blame for everything. I got her into trouble and I'd do anything to get her out. I'd go through anything. I'd give you anything. I'd even give you my own life. I really mean it. I really do. I know that you can do it, too. Save my sister, *and take me instead*!'

12

RED MIST

I came to myself to find that I was huddled against an upturned tree root, covered with a blanket of snow. I had no idea that I was on Plynlimon, and certainly no memory of that strange white house. Pawl's old, black flapping coat was pulled round me, and my body was curled up tight. On every side lay open moorland and, as far as I was concerned, I'd just survived a night sleeping rough in the sort of conditions that should have taken my life.

I sat up slowly, stiff all over. It was a dark day, with not a hint of sunshine anywhere. But at least I'm alive, I thought. I should be dead, and yet I'm not. I've got through a whole night out in the open, and somehow I've survived!

In the distance, I could hear bells ringing. My sense of achievement was so great that I actually felt as if they were ringing for me. For a moment, I sat listening to them, but then my thoughts returned to Cary, and everything came crashing down.

It was like waking from a bad dream only to find

that real life was worse. Yesterday I'd started out for Pengwern, but I'd lost my way and now a whole day had been wasted. I staggered to my feet, and set off again through the snow, not knowing where I was going but praying that I'd somehow manage to find the road that I'd been looking for the day before.

The moorland fell behind me and I slipped into the forest. Tall trees surrounded me, weighed down with snow. The bells stopped ringing, not a creature stirred and silence fell. The forest was in a sombre mood. I hummed to keep up my spirits, but it was an impossible task. I didn't like this deep, quiet forest. Fingers of mist worked their way towards me, and I didn't like them either.

In the end, I broke into a run. I felt as if something was stalking me, stealthy and determined, like an unwanted memory. A huge black crow went winging through the forest, crabbing like a grumpy old man whose morning lie-in has been ruined. The echo of its complaint lingered long after it had gone.

I ran and ran, but the mist reached out for me – and it was winning, hands down. I couldn't get away from it, and the coldness that it brought was like the presence of ghosts. I felt them gathering, like a haunting. Saw shapes in the mist, and heard a little moaning noise that sounded like the whine of dogs.

By this time, I was running full pelt. But the more I ran, the more the mist wrapped itself around me. There was nothing I could do to shake it off. Even when I found a snowplough in the forest, digging a path through the snow, there was no hope of rescue. I waved and yelled as its yellow flashing light disappeared between the trees, but its driver never saw me. I caught a glimpse of him laughing to himself, as if he loved the forest and was a happy man, but then the mist came down between us and he was gone.

I was on my own again – and something very nasty was coming after me. By this time, I could see shapes in the mist – mottled coats and pale eyes, and I could hear a panting sound as well, growing steadily closer. I pressed on, heart thundering, legs buckling, thinking that I'd had it, and might as well give up.

I don't know what I would have done if a small black cat hadn't popped up in front of me and become my rescuer. There it suddenly was, right in front of me. It saw the strange misty creatures coming after me and shot off through the trees, luring them away. The creatures were fast, but the cat knew the forest better than they did. You could see that from the way it wove a path between the trees, playing 'catch me if you can'.

Finally it disappeared, and its pursuers disappeared as well, taking the mist with them. Slowly I began to make out trees again, and the sky above them. I saw the snowy forest floor. Saw the sun shining down long avenues of spruce and pine, and saw the valley down below them.

That was when it came to me that I was on Plynlimon Mountain. I stopped in my tracks and stared at the valley. I didn't understand. Birds sang in the clear sky. A little breeze blew against my face. The sun caught particles of snow and made them sparkle as if the very air itself was made of silver.

I can't be on Plynlimon, I thought. How could I ever have got here? But then I saw a gate, and Clockvine House was behind it, and I was on

Plynlimon, no two ways about it. I mightn't know how come, but this was where I was.

I hurried towards the house, imagining hot baths, hot food, dry clothes and a journey back to the village in the Katterfeltos' tour bus. It was then that I saw my rescuer again. He was lying on the drive. One of his ears had been torn off, and his face was full of blood. I cried out in horror but, as soon as I moved towards him, the small black cat got up and limped away as if afraid of me. He hid in the stable-block, down the side of the Katterfeltos' tour bus. I went after him, pushing my way into the darknesss, calling, 'Come on, come on, it's all right. It's only me.'

And there they all were, waiting for me! My shadowy pursuers. They were everywhere. Between the stalls, behind the bus, in the deepest darkest corners – even hanging in the air! The place was full of them. Great grey dogs, with burning eyes that told me what I should have known already – that they were the *Cŵn y Wbir*!

'No!' I whispered, looking for the cat, as if the two of us were in this together and together we would stand. But the cat walked away. It wouldn't look at me. It sauntered off, without a limp. And then I knew.

This was a trap.

I'd been set up.

I'd been served up, like dinner on a plate!

All around me, I heard dogs panting, and felt their hunger in the air, as thick as lust. A lust to kill. *And suddenly I felt that lust as well!*

In the past, I'd always seen black when I lost my temper – a black cloud would come over me and everything would seem to throb. But this time I saw red. It started at the corners of my vision and rolled inwards like a mist. Everything was hazy; everything was indistinct. The only thing I could see clearly was the small black cat as it picked its way across the stable yard, getting out before things started turning nasty. It was a prissy cat. It was fastidious. It had had its bit of fun, but it didn't want to stick around for the kill.

And suddenly I hated it. I wished it dead. The dogs were closing in on me, but all I could think about was the cat. It had done this to me. Tricked me, and played with me, and lured me here. And, if it was the last thing I ever did, *I had to pay it back.*

Pay it back?

I HAD TO KILL IT!

It wasn't hard to do. My weapon was at hand – a mallet hanging from a nail. I snatched it up, swung it over my head, and never afterwards would I be able to claim that I didn't know what I was doing. For I knew perfectly. I knew it in every muscle, bone and sinew of my body as the mallet flew down the stable like a guided missile, and my voice flew after it, yelling, '*Go to hell!*'

13

THE CONJUROR'S REVENGE

The red mist cleared inside my head, as if the words I'd shouted and the thing I'd done had killed it dead. On the ground in front of me lay Gilda Katterfelto. She, too, was dead. A pool of blood spread out from her head. The cat had gone – *I mean, there was no cat* – and there were no dogs either. The stable-block was empty except for Dr Katterfelto's tour bus, and so was the drive beyond it. The dogs had disappeared, leaving not a trace behind.

I leant against an old stall, feeling sick. Daylight was fading beyond the stable door, but I could still see what I'd done. I looked at Gilda's eyes, which had filled up with blood. Looked at the place where the mallet had smashed into her head and, like a drunk waking from a rampage, couldn't quite believe that it was anything to do with me.

There are things you never want to think about. Moments that you don't ever want to revisit but, for all your trying, they still haunt you. Well, this is one of those for me. Sometimes it wakes me still in a panic. I feel the way I did then, sick and giddy, falling over an abyss with nothing underneath me. Falling through darkness. I remember the awfulness of picking up Gilda's body and dragging it under the tour bus, telling myself that nobody would find it there, not for days.

Not until I'd got away.

It was a senseless thing to do, of course – completely crazy, just like everything else. For there could be no hiding what I'd done. Dr Katterfelto would know something was wrong the moment Gilda failed to return indoors. Even if he missed the blood on the stable floor – even if he failed, at first, to see my weasel footsteps sneaking off through the snow – he'd know that something was terribly wrong.

Later, I felt horror at what I'd done. But, at the time, I was in shock. I remember telling myself that a madman must be lurking about, having done this terrible thing, or a convict on the run or a burglar. I must have known that it was me, but I tore out of that stable block and off down the mountain as if whoever had done this thing might get me next.

Looking back, that entire journey is wiped from my mind. All I can remember is suddenly seeing the rooftops of the village ahead of me, lit by a clear sky. I slipped down the pass road into the village, telling myself that if I could only make it back to Prospect House then I'd be safe.

But I was fooling myself. I would never be safe again. I had changed, and my world had changed with me. Even Prospect House had changed, as if something subtle and catastrophic had happened to it. As it had, of course – and that something was *me*.

For ever afterwards, Prospect House would be notorious. A shadow would hang over it. It would be the birthplace of that famous local murderer, Zachary Fitztalbot. For that was who I was, and that was what I'd done. It hadn't been a madman or a convict or a burglar who'd killed Gilda Katterfelto.

It was me.

Finally the full horror hit home. I imagined policemen coming after me with cars and helicopters and guns. Imagined my parents never speaking to me again as they died a thousand deaths of social shame. Imagined the village turning its back on me, and Pawl turning his face away, and even Grace turning in her grave, ashamed to share the same blood.

But worse than all of that – *worse by far* – I imagined Gilda Katterfelto being dead. I'd taken everything from her, from the way she tucked her hair into her green silk cap to the sparkle in her emerald eyes. She'd never again help her father with his magic shows, or bow to him as if he was the undisputed master. I'd taken that from him, as well. Taken it from both of them, along with everything Gilda might have done, or felt or been. I'd taken her whole life – and there was nothing I could do to bring it back.

I'll have to give myself up, I thought, standing outside Prospect House, looking up at its dark windows. I'll have to make a confession to the police. There's no way I can hide a thing like this. Anyone who sees me will know what I've done. They'll see it in my eyes. See it written all over me. I can't escape from it.

I entered the house, determined to do the deed straightaway, before I changed my mind. Before I could get halfway down the hall, however, I saw a dark figure sitting on the stairs. I didn't need to switch on the lights to know that it was Dr Katterfelto – and that he was waiting for me.

He stared at me, and I stared back, wondering how on earth he'd done that – found his daughter's body underneath the bus, and put two and two together and come up with me, and then got down the mountain to the village ahead of me.

But that was what he'd done, and now his wait was over. He rose to his feet, and I started to stutter stupid words that wouldn't come out right, and made no difference anyway. For Dr Katterfelto hadn't come to hear me stumble over the word 'sorry', no matter how many times I tried to get it out. Nor had he come for the assurance that I was just about to hand myself in. He hadn't come for anything that I might do in my attempts to make amends.

He'd come to get me!

To take the law into his own hands.

To punish me.

One look at his face, and I knew that I was done for. I turned tail and fled the house, knowing that there'd be no point in pleading for my life. I slammed the front door behind me, and the gate as well, gaining precious seconds, then headed down the lane in the direction of the bridge.

But Dr Katterfelto was right behind me. I slid down the side of the bridge and headed off across the meadow, but couldn't shake him off. I tried to stay ahead, but didn't stand a chance. I was too weary, and he was too fast. Finally he made a grab for me and held on tight. I tried to break away, and suddenly it was like a strange Christmas pantomime, full of mime but without the jokes. Not a word was said between us. Dr Katterfelto got me by the shoulders and dragged me to the water's edge. I fought him desperately, but he was extraordinarily strong and I couldn't escape.

Finally I stopped struggling. I was certain that Dr Katterfelto was going to drown me but there was nothing I could do to stop him. I hung in his arms, knowing that whatever happened next, I deserved it.

'Let me show you one last wonder!' Dr Katterfelto hissed, lifting my face up close to his. 'One last trick before we part ways – and I'm sure that you'll agree it's *my best yet*!'

His eyes burned into me like twin fires. I couldn't get away from them but, the more I looked, the stranger I felt. I couldn't think straight, couldn't move and, in the end, couldn't even breathe. I needed air, but couldn't get it. My face felt hot, and my body started pouring with sweat.

I knew I had to break away, but couldn't move a muscle. I couldn't even feel my heartbeat any more. It was as if a coup was taking place, imprisoning my body inside my mind. I know that doesn't make much sense, but that's the only way I can explain it.

And that's the way that Dr Katterfelto wanted it. 'Now you're mine,' he hissed. 'All mine. Your life in my hands, just like Gilda's was in yours. What does it feel like? Can you tell me? Come on, say something. Don't just stand there like a lump of wood!'

But that was what I felt like. A lump of wood. I stared at the doctor, and my arms felt like winter branches on a dead tree, my feet like a pair of gnarled, old, twisted roots and my fingers sapless and skeletal, like last year's leaves. Worse still, when I looked into the doctor's eyes, all I could see was a dead old tree. No sign of me. No reflection of Zachary.

Just a tree.

As if he knew what I could see, the doctor smiled. And then I understood. It surely wasn't possible, and yet he'd done it. The famous Dr Katterfelto – undisputed master of village halls and palaces – *had turned me into a tree.*

'Now you know what sorry means,' he said, taking a low bow, as if I was his best trick ever. 'You know it right down in your bones. What a marvel I've created! What a wonder you are! They should try a little hocus pocus when they want to punish murderers. It'd save a lot of trouble. Clear the backlog in the courts and cut down on man-hours and expense. And what wonderful results! For every evil, killing bastard, a beautiful tree!

'You should thank me, Zachary Fitztalbot. For the first time in your life, people will look up to you. They'll stop to shelter in your shade, rest beneath your branches, picnic under you and even carve their love-hearts in your skin. You'll have a use at last, instead of being a waste of space. *You'll have a purpose to your miserable life!*'

He turned to go, leaving me behind. It was the bitterest of nights, and getting colder all the time. Everything was glittering, from the stars in the sky to the Afon Gwy, which was freezing over. It was the sort of frost you read about in books – the sort that people tell tall tales about and never forget. The sort where people die.

I tried, deep down inside, to cry for help, but not a sound came out. Dr Katterfelto turned back once, to take a final look. His eyes were cruel, entirely without pity. I knew that, when he'd gone, I would remember them. I'd stand here like this, rooted to the spot, and the triumph in his eyes would remain with me for ever. It was his parting gift. It was the conjuror's revenge.

14

CRYSTAL NIGHT

Above me shone more stars than I had ever seen in my life, and beneath them the valley sparkled with a frost that covered everything like a second layer of snow. Rooftops glittered as if made of jewels, and St Curig's church spire looked like a silver space rocket pointing to the sky. The Afon Gwy looked silver too, but no longer did it run down the valley chattering on its way. Instead it was frozen over from one side to the other. Frozen and immobile, going nowhere.

Just like me.

By now, my feet were one with the river bank, frozen to it, never to move again. My blood was frozen in my veins, and my eyes were choked with crystals that confused my vision, forcing me to see as if through a prism. Everything I looked at seemed broken into pieces. Nothing looked whole any more.

Even the distant outline of Plynlimon looked like a jumble of shapes, rising from the valley floor like an abstract painting. It was hard to believe that I'd ever found myself up on that mountain, not knowing how

I'd got there. What an ending this had turned out to be, after all my efforts to return to Pengwern!

The night grew colder all the time. Birds froze on their roosts, dying where they slept. I would have given anything to die as well. To deep-freeze fast and get it done with. But, oh no, I had to linger on, feeling the coldness eating into me.

Sometime in the night, I heard a distant sound of singing. I couldn't see a soul but, as the thin notes drifted my way, I realised that I was listening to a carol. *Midnights clear* came drifting my way, and *harps of gold*, and *peace on earth* and *wings unfurled*. At first none of it made any sense at all, but then I saw lights on in St Curig's church, and realised that it was Christmas Eve.

Happy Christmas, Zed! I thought. I couldn't have felt more sorry for myself. In the distance, I could see tiny figures coming out of church and heading off into the darkness. One of them was Pawl's. He climbed on to his sled and headed for home, pulled by Harri and Mari.

I watched him all the way. When he drew level with the tin house, instead of turning down the bank, he carried on. It was as if he couldn't find his home, and was searching for it. He reached the bridge and started down its side and across the meadow. I wished that he could see me. Wished that I could do something to attract his attention. The sled crossed the frozen river, right in front of me, then turned round and came back, Pawl grinning and waving as if my wish had come true.

When I didn't wave back, he started calling. 'What do you ... think you're doing ... standing there with

… your arms in … the air don't … look at me … like that Zed … are you all … right what are … you playing at?' he called.

How did Pawl know that I was Zed? I stared at him woodenly, and he stared back as if my identity was obvious. Again he asked what I was doing and, when I still didn't answer, he drew the sled round in front of me and started frowning like a cross child.

'You can't just … stand there help … yourself come on … don't be so … stupid pull yourself … together Zed stop … playing stupid games …' he said.

Still I didn't answer, and then Pawl started getting angry. He got down from the sled and came stomping through the snow to thrust his scowling face into mine and breathe clouds of white breath all over me. I still couldn't figure out how he knew who I was, but now even Harri and Mari were staring as if my identity was an open secret.

'What's wrong is … something up with … you why won't … you move has … someone hypnotised you?' he shouted into my face.

He didn't mean it, of course. It was just a figure of speech. But then Pawl started shaking me as well and, in his eyes, I saw myself reflected. Only it wasn't the new me that I saw. Wasn't the Zed who'd been turned into a tree. It was the old me – and, as soon as I saw it, I knew that Pawl was right.

I *have* been hypnotised! I thought. I only think I'm a tree, but I'm not really. It's just a trick on the doctor's part. Sleight-of-hand and sleight-of-mind. All just an illusion. *Dr Katterfelto's played a trick on me.*

Inside myself, anger started rising. No matter what I'd done to Gilda, I didn't deserve this. Even murderers deserved justice – and this was as far from justice as anything could be.

Pawl stopped shaking, and tried to pick me up. I must have been a dead weight, because he failed. Don't think you'll get away with this, I raged silently against the doctor. Don't think that you can fool me. You haven't got a hold on me. My heart can beat all on its own, and I can breathe, and think, and feel and be. Right here, right now, I'm doing it – and you can't stop me. Do you hear? You think you can, but really *you can't touch me*!

It did the trick, too. Deep down inside myself, I felt the doctor lose his grip. Felt it like a straightjacket working loose. Suddenly my frozen body was melting, my muscles unknotting and my mind working free. My heart began to beat properly, and the blood to pump again. My fingers moved, and my arms dropped to my sides. My feet came back to life. I blinked away the crystals and looked Pawl straight in the eye.

Immediately his scowl melted, and he gave me a big hug. I was back, and he could see it. He tore the hat off his head and the coat off his back and put them on me. Then he half-carried, half-led me to the sled, settled me on the high bench seat, jumped up beside me, and we set off up the meadow towards the village.

The dogs pulled the sled with all the strength of a pair of pack-horses. I lay back and closed my eyes. Tomorrow I'd have to deal with what I'd done to Gilda. It wouldn't go away. I'd have to explain to Pawl about Dr Katterfelto, and what he'd done to me and why. I'd also have to give myself up to the police, and my parents would be dragged in. And then nothing in my life would ever be the same!

'One day you'll *really* get yourself in trouble!' my mother had always said. But, this time, it wouldn't just be my father that I'd have to deal with. It would be the full force of justice in the courts of law.

For tonight, however, I sank back into what felt like the world's most welcome rest, listening to the sound of silver runners racing over the snow. To me it was the sound of life itself, wrapped around me like a child's comfort blanket, welcoming me home from the strange land of the dead.

15

MEMORIES

I was surprised that Pawl took me back to his place, but relieved as well because I didn't know how I'd face Prospect House with the memory of Dr Katterfelto waiting on the stairs. The sled drew round the back and came to a halt in a small yard surrounded by sheds. Pawl unharnessed the dogs and gave me a hand down. I was astonished at how weak I was when I tried to stand. He had to lift me down and carry me inside.

The tin house was much bigger than anyone would expect from the outside, and it was homelier as well. I'd hardly ever been inside because, for all his friendliness, Pawl was a private man who rarely invited anyone in. Outside it was just a shack in need of paint, but inside it was warm and cosy, and smelt of Christmas cooking. It was tidy as well – never a virtue that anyone would associate with a man who mostly wore his clothes inside out and back to front – everything in its place, and everything carefully labelled.

Pawl dug out logs from a basket labelled 'Fuel', and coaxed his wood-burning stove back to life. Then he pulled up a sofa and settled me on it with a hot-water bottle, labelled 'Hot Water – Careful – Do Not Boil' and a blanket labelled 'Spare Room'. He drew the curtains against the night, poked the fire until flames went leaping up the stove-pipe, and brought me a supper of turkey sandwiches and Christmas cake, served on a tray labelled 'Pantry – Second Shelf'.

I stuffed it all down – even the marzipan on the Christmas cake, which I had never liked, but now it tasted wonderful. It was the first time in days that I had eaten properly and, when I'd finished, I felt exhausted. I lay back against a pile of cushions, basking like a sleepy fish in sunny waters. It was as much as I could do to keep myself from falling asleep right there and then, but Pawl had made a proper bed for me upstairs and wanted me to sleep in it.

He was obviously very proud of what he had achieved at a moment's notice, turning an unused junk room into a welcoming guest bedroom. I said how nice it was, and fell into bed. Pawl tucked me in as if I was a baby, announcing that he would leave me in peace.

In the doorway, however, he turned back. There was one final thing that he had remembered. 'Good news about ... Cary getting better ... don't you think ... turned a corner ... best Christmas present ... in the world ...' he said.

'*Getting better?*' I said.

Pawl nodded. 'Yes,' he said.

I should have been thrilled – in fact, I should have been ecstatic – but I found myself shivering as if a chill wind had blown into my life. Pawl disappeared before I could ask for details. I could have gone rushing after him, but something held me back. I lay in bed, blaming tiredness for the strange mood that had descended upon me. But I wasn't tired enough to get to sleep.

I lay awake for ages. Long after Pawl himself had gone to bed, I was still awake. Up the valley somewhere, farm dogs barked in a shed. Downstairs in the kitchen, Harri and Mari whined. I shivered under my covers.

Once I would have lain awake waiting for Santa on a night like this, I thought, but now I don't know what I'm waiting for.

I fell asleep in the end, but awoke before first light to hear Harri and Mari still whining in the kitchen. What was the matter with them? I looked out of the window to see if everything was all right. The yard was empty, and so was the bank up to the lane but, off in the night somewhere, I could hear those farm dogs again. It seemed to me that they were closer now. I stood listening to them crying in the darkness, and disturbing half-memories started coming back – shapes in the mist, and being chased, and other things too, which felt like the remains of a nightmare: strange white houses, and darkened rooms, and stubs of candles burning without giving any light.

In the end, to shake them off, I went downstairs. Harri and Mari looked up as I entered the kitchen. 'It's all right,' I told them. 'Don't look like that. Everything's fine. It's just that I can't sleep, that's all.'

I gave them both a hug and wished them Happy Christmas. But if it was Christmas morning, then why had Pawl cooked his turkey a day early? I caught sight of its carcass in the pantry, and saw the Christmas cake he'd started too, and the beers he'd opened, with 'Alcohol – Christmas – 25th', written on their carrier. Then I saw a roasting pan in the kitchen sink as well, and discarded wrapping paper in the bin, as if Pawl had opened his presents a day early.

I stooped and got it out, smoothed it down and read the labels, telling myself that yet again poor old Pawl had got his days mixed up. But what if *I* was mixed up, not him? What if my strange half-memories were trying to tell me that I'd lost a day? My mind went back to the sound of bells on the mountain. I'd thought they rang for my survival, but what if they'd rung for Christmas Day instead, and something had happened to me on that mountain – *something that I wanted to forget?*

'No,' I said. 'I'm being ridiculous. It isn't possible!'

I turned to leave the kitchen, as if to shake off my nameless fears. But suddenly a small room came to mind, and I remembered someone there with me in the darkness, and felt their presence. Then all sorts of things came flooding back, words and memories that I couldn't contain:

'I'd do anything ... I'd go through anything ... I'd give you anything ... even my own life ... take me instead.'

Now I said the words again, like an actor repeating lines. And I knew them all by heart, *because the words were mine!*

I *said* them, I thought. I really did. It wasn't a dream. It actually happened. I was trapped there in that room – *and I know who by!*

I started flying about the kitchen, grabbing everything I'd need to make a getaway. I had to escape, and I had to do it fast. For it was payback time. I'd struck a deal with the red judge, and he'd kept his side of the bargain – and now he'd sent his *Cŵn y Wbir* to collect!

In the biggest panic ever, I grabbed food, drink, warm clothes, blankets and anything else that came to hand, including Pawl's big black coat hanging on the back door. He wouldn't mind, I told myself – not if he knew the danger I was in. I hauled it all outside, piled it into Grace's sled, tied it down with a tarpaulin and then hugged Harri and Mari, who stood in the doorway as if they couldn't figure out what was going on, telling them that they couldn't come with me, and this was farewell. Then I got behind the sled, and tried to push it off. But it was frozen to the yard, and wouldn't budge. No matter how hard I tried, I couldn't break it out.

In the end, Harri and Mari had to help me. They did a magnificent job, too, harnessed to the sled and breaking it free as if they were old hands, straining first to one side, then the other, then lunging forward so that it came shooting out of the ice.

I had to run behind to catch them up. They pulled the sled up the bank to the lane, and would have carried on, too, if I hadn't made them stop. I thanked them and went to undo their harnesses, but they looked at me as if I was mad. I hadn't really meant that this was farewell, their eyes seemed to say. Surely I knew that they wanted to come too? They'd caught a whiff of something blowing up the valley – a promise of adventure that they couldn't resist.

'No,' I said. 'You can't. *We* can't. You're Pawl's. He needs you. You can't come with me. You've got to go home.'

I glanced back at the tin house, afraid of Pawl seeing what was going on. And there he was, sure enough, standing at his bedroom window, holding back the curtain as if he'd seen it all. I went again to unharness the dogs, but he waved a hand as if to say, 'No, no, off you go. It's fine by me. *I understand*.'

Then he stepped back from the window and let the curtain drop. I knew he'd never tell a soul about what he'd seen. I mightn't understand why, but suddenly I knew that there was more to Pawl than met the eye. I'd always felt that there was, but now I'd seen it for myself.

I waved my hand as well, wishing that I knew him better, but guessing that I never would. Then I climbed on to the high bench seat, and we set off. The tin house fell behind us. I watched it disappearing. Harri and Mari pulled the sled down the side of the bridge, then started along the frozen Afon Gwy as if it were a six-lane highway. There were no signposts to direct them, but who needs signposts?

Plynlimon lay behind me, and the river lay ahead. I knew that if I kept on course then I'd be safe. Nobody would ever find me, not even the red judge. I shivered at the thought of it – shivered with excitement. My journey stretched ahead of me all the way to the sea. I felt it waiting like the gateway to a whole new life.

16

MY SEAFARING FATHER

The time has come to tell you about my other father. I'm not talking about my real father here, who was dead, or my Fitztalbot father, who was best forgotten. I'm talking about the father I made up for myself when I didn't have anybody else. The one I called my 'seafaring father'.

He's the reason why, that morning, knowing that the sea lay waiting for me up ahead meant so very much. I made him up when I first moved to Pengwern. Faced with the awful reality of my new Fitztalbot father, I started fantasising about the sort of father that I'd really like. Over time, I polished him up until I got him just the way I wanted. Then – when he was perfect – I believed in him.

I know it must sound crazy but, for years, he was so real that if I'd met him on the street I would have known him. He was just like me – a rebel too, who hated school and uniforms and being made to keep the rules; someone who ran away to sea when he was scarcely my age, and who understood me so well that when I looked at him, I couldn't help but understand myself.

I saw my dreams fulfilled in him. For years, I imagined running away and finding him waiting when I got to the sea, tanned by the wind, dark-haired, tough and wiry, and as handsome as a gypsy. '*Life's for living, not keeping shop.*' That was one of his favourite sayings, as made up by me. '*You're only as good as the storms you have survived.*' That was another – and he knew what he was talking about!

My seafaring father had seen it all – waves as tall as skyscrapers, and nights on seas so calm that you couldn't tell where the sky ended and the sea began. He'd fought with pirates and found treasure islands. Met fabled beasts and ghost ships. Survived storms the likes of which most people could never imagine. His tales were tall and wild – and I always believed them, even though I was the one who'd made them up.

That's the one important thing I want to get across. Even though I made him up, I still believed in my seafaring father. It was like believing in the future. Having hope against all odds. One day, I told myself, the two of us would go off together across the seven seas. We'd do battle with wild storms and always win. Drink ourselves silly in every port. Share girls together – legendary lovers, father and son. There'd be nothing I couldn't achieve with him by my side, and nothing he wouldn't do for me.

He was twice as alive as anybody else. He wasn't like my real father, who had gone and died. And he certainly wasn't like my Fitztalbot father, who didn't know what it meant to live. Even as I grew older and stopped thinking about him so much, I still knew that he was out there on the high seas, waiting for the day when I would join him.

And now that day had come! My head knew that my seafaring father wasn't real, but my heart told me that he'd be waiting when I got downriver to the sea. Here I was facing yet another unexpected, new and highly uncertain life, and there he was, waiting for me like he always had done.

Suddenly the journey took on a whole new light. I wasn't running *from* something any more, but *to* something instead. Morning broke across the sky. It lit the tops of all the hills, but I refused to look back. It was too bright a morning for looking back, and the world ahead was too exciting. The air was clear and blue, as if the atmosphere had been stretched out thin. The sun rose in a perfect sky and my spirits rose as well. I felt them soaring through the air. Felt like a bird flying down the river.

I've done it, I thought. I've got away. The *Cŵn y Wbir* won't catch me, and neither will their master. I'm shaking off his shadow, and I'm free of him. Free of everybody else as well who ever tried to put me down!

It was a moment of sheer exhilaration. Completely unexpectedly, the future was suddenly bright. I'd tricked the red judge into saving Cary's life, then slipped through his fingers and got away with it.

Suddenly I felt free. Old landscapes fell behind me and new ones appeared. Harri and Mari drew the sled down a long, narrowing valley, their muscles working like the Furies underneath their shaggy coats. I didn't have to drive them, or tell them where to go. They ran as if our destinations were the same.

Cliffs started closing in on us, and the sun disappeared. We entered a gorge with heavy woodland on either side. Shadows fell across the sled, but I didn't feel cast down by them. I felt safe, as if the cliffs were strong arms holding the world at bay.

Even when Harri and Mari stopped at last, and couldn't go any further, I still felt safe. In front of the sled lay a jumble of boulders, fallen tree-trunks and plates of ice, frozen together to create thick wedge-like steps. There was no way forward, apart from picking our way down them slowly, but I didn't care. The gorge was too beautiful to mind slowing down. In the icy morning, it was like a treasure chest stuffed full of jewels.

I could have rummaged through it for days, marvelling over silver branches, frozen leaves, ferns laced with snow and cobwebs beaded like pearl necklaces. Every one of them looked priceless – a treasure beyond measure. By the time the river smoothed out again, I was sad to say goodbye. The cliffs fell back and the end of the gorge was in sight. I felt the sun on my face again, and looked up to see it high in the sky.

The day was moving on – and so must we. I climbed back on to the sled, and Harri and Mari started running again. The gorge fell behind us and I caught a glimpse of a winding road that I recognised as the Rhayader road. Usually it was busy with Land Rovers and trailers taking sheep and cattle to market, but today it was snowed over.

Even so, I didn't want to go through Rhayader. I was afraid of being recognised as Grace's grandson, and even more afraid that the word might be out and the town would be looking for a murderer. Before I could do anything about it, however, Rhayader was upon me. It was busy too, the riverbank crowded with people enjoying the whitest Christmas holiday for years. The park was packed beneath the ruined castle, and crowds walked along its paths, marvelling at what the freak weather conditions had done. Nobody who'd seen how fast the river flowed around this town could quite believe that it had frozen over. And nobody who knew how dangerous it could be would ever venture on to the ice.

'Hey, you!' they shouted when the sled glided into view. 'Get off that ice! Stop mucking about! Stop playing the fool!'

They waved at me, as if they thought I couldn't hear, and a couple of them even threw stones. I was being irresponsible, they shouted, risking the dogs' lives as well as my own. I couldn't get past them quickly enough, and neither could Harri and Mari. They broke into a trot and the sled shot round a long bend in the river, following the line of a wooded cliff until the voices faded at last.

I'm glad that's over, I thought as the sled slowed down.

But it wasn't over yet. Before I had the time to savour my relief, a tall stone bridge appeared. It stood high above the river and was crowded with yet more people who, at the sight of us, all started shouting too. We disappeared under its arches, and came out the other side to a chorus of cries of 'Get back!' and 'Mind the edge!'

But what edge? Harri and Mari pulled the sled across a frozen pool of water that had formed itself into a perfect skating rink, with nobody on it except for us. They couldn't see any danger, and neither could I. 'Mind the edge!' people shouted again, but we still didn't see anything – not until it was suddenly too late. One minute we were hurrying along, looking forward to getting away, and the next we were tumbling over a short but rocky waterfall that separated the high town from the lower one.

It wasn't a long fall, but it certainly wasn't a pleasant one. The dogs went first, shooting down a series of icy gullies and landing on the frozen river at the bottom. Then the sled came after them, crashing with such force that I don't know how it stayed in one piece. Then I came last of all, slamming on to the ice and lying there in pain, dimly aware that I could hear myself crying.

I couldn't move, and at first I thought I must be unconscious. But then I remember seeing our provisions scattered all over the ice. They were out of reach, and I didn't know what to do about them. I lay there feeling helpless, watching Harri and Mari pick themselves up as if crashing down waterfalls was all in a day's work, shake themselves down and somehow manage to right the sled, untwisting its harness and getting ready to set off again.

They were amazing. All I had to do was get to my feet, gather up what provisions I could and get back on board. Then we were off again, hurrying away before anybody came rushing down from the high town to see if we were all right. We were sore, but at least we'd survived. We'd got away with it, no bones broken and the sled intact.

But, after that, nothing felt quite the same. I kept

telling myself that it could have been worse, but I no longer felt like the person who'd set out that morning. I wasn't fearless any more, as if nothing could get me. I didn't feel quite so free. Round every bend, I realised, you could never tell what would happen next.

I started looking behind me, as if afraid of being followed, then searching the riverbanks ahead of me for evidence of the sea. I knew I shouldn't expect the river to be tidal yet, but I couldn't help myself. The sun began to sink, and Harri and Mari started slowing down at last, their fabulous energy finally wearing thin. We stopped to eat, and I discovered how many of our provisions I'd left behind on the ice. I counted what was missing and cursed myself for my stupidity. There was only enough food left for the next day – two at the most.

'We'll have to carry on,' I told the dogs. 'I'm sorry, but we can't afford to stop. We've hardly anything to eat, and it's got to last until we get to the sea.'

We started off again, heading downriver in the darkness. A little wind got up, moaning behind us like a police-car siren on a murder hunt. I told myself that I was imagining it – that the night was playing tricks. But I felt as if the shadow of Plynlimon was reaching out for me.

I shivered on my high bench-seat, pulling as many blankets round me as I could reach. Slowly we drew round a great bend in the river until a few lights came into view. I looked at them, wishing that they could be the lights of Pengwern, and that the last few days could have been a dream and I could have my old life back again.

Suddenly I wanted everything back the way it had been before Cary came home with that light bulb stuck to her head. It mightn't have been the best of lives, but at least it had been safe. I wanted Cary to be her old self. I wanted my mother. I wanted our house on Swan Hill. I wanted my bed.

Oh, how I wanted my bed!

Crouching on the high bench seat, shivering despite the blankets, I thought of flannel sheets and feather pillows, pyjamas warming in the airing cupboard, cocoa and hot-water bottles. I thought of radiators throwing out obscene amounts of heat, curtains pulled against the night, bed socks and furry slippers, dressing gowns and electric blankets.

And, suddenly, it was too much for me. I can't go on, I thought. I can't do this. I'm not a seven seas adventurer. Not ready for a new life. I want to stop this happening. Turn back the clock. Open my eyes and find I'm back in Pengwern!

By now we were level with the lights, which belonged to a tiny hamlet. I looked at cars on drives and smoking chimney pots, streetlights, pub lights and glimpses between curtains of television screens. And it was only a short distance, in my mind, from wanting Pengwern back again to thinking that I'd got it.

'I'm home,' I told myself. 'I'm back. I know I am. I can see it. I'm not imagining it. Not making it up. I've returned to Pengwern. This is what I asked for. It's what I need. Now I can put the past behind me. Start again. Start afresh. It's time to pull myself together. But, first of all ...

'It's time for bed!'

I tried to steer Harri and Mari off the ice but, as if

they knew that I'd gone funny in the head, they refused to budge. They were heading downriver, and nothing could persuade them to change direction. Even when I promised them a good hot dinner in my mother's kitchen, they wouldn't budge. Even when I promised fire and bed.

So I left them where they were – stuck there on the ice – and headed home alone.

17

LLEWELLYN'S CAVE

It didn't take me long to realise that I'd got it wrong about Pengwern. I didn't find my bed, for all my trudging through the snow, but I did find something else and, after all this time, I still remember it as clearly as ever.

I found it on the far side of the hamlet, in a moonlit field bordered by trees. I'd been following a road that ended on a dead-end track, and was trying to work my way back to the river in the hope of catching up with Harri and Mari. Streetlights glimmered in the distance, but I was so cold and confused that I couldn't figure out how to get to them.

It was a stupid muddle to get into, going round in circles on the sort of night when anyone with any sense was tucked up tight indoors. I pulled Pawl's coat tightly round me, but it made no difference. I was so cold that I couldn't even breathe without pain. My legs dragged, my arms hung like lumps of lead and nothing worked properly any more – especially my brain!

Nothing made sense. I couldn't figure out where I'd come from, and I certainly couldn't figure out where I was heading – not until I discovered a set of footprints in the snow. They could have been mine for all I knew but, to my confused brain, they looked like a map pointing the way. So I started following them, telling myself that I'd be all right because somebody had gone this way before me.

I was desperate for company. That was the thing. Desperate for somebody to take charge of me and keep me safe. I wanted someone now, and the footsteps gave me hope.

I followed them across first one field then another. But I didn't find anybody, and all too soon I was in a state of collapse. Then it started snowing again – great white flakes that covered everything, including me. I crossed a frozen stream and started up the slope of a low, wooded cliff. Then the footprints disappeared, and I didn't have even them any more.

It was in this state that I saw the cave. Suddenly there it was in front of me, its rocky entrance half-hidden by trees. I almost fell into it with relief. My head banged on its roof as I stooped to enter, but I didn't care. All that mattered was that I'd found a place of shelter.

I worked my way into its darkness, looking for a draught-free corner where the wind wouldn't blow in and the snow wouldn't cover me. The cave roof got lower all the way down, and I ended up crawling on hands and knees. But I found the corner that I was looking for, and even found a bed of leaves. It wasn't exactly the bed that I'd hoped for when I'd left the river, but it was better than nothing.

Finally I gave myself permission to collapse. I didn't expect to sleep, but exhaustion overwhelmed me and I dropped straight off. I even managed to dream – although I rather wished I hadn't, because I found myself being chased by half the people I'd ever known, including my Fitztalbot relatives headed by my grandmother, who might look like a wizened old prune but, boy, could she run!

I woke up in a panic, shot up with a jolt and bumped my head. At first I saw stars but, after they'd gone, a source of light still remained. The cave walls flickered, and I realised I was warm and wasn't shivering any more.

What was going on here? I looked into the light, only to discover that I was no longer alone. A figure sat in the cave's entrance, feeding a camp fire with twigs and leaves. His head turned slowly, and our eyes met. I looked at slits of silver, and a face so tight and tired that it could barely keep awake. But his smile was warm and genuine, and it made me feel safe.

'You all right?' said a lilting voice that, as far as I was concerned, could only be Welsh.

'I'm fine,' I said. And suddenly I felt fine too. I hadn't died of hypothermia, as I could so easily have done, and my bad dream had gone. I even had a fire to keep me warm, and the company that I had craved. Things could definitely be worse.

I lay down again and fell back to sleep. Every time I awoke throughout the rest of the night, the figure was still there, sitting in the cave entrance where nothing could get past him, staring into the night as if keeping the darkness at bay.

In the morning, however, he was gone. I awoke to

find the fire burned out, leaving only ashes. I crawled outside to see if anybody was there, but the cliff was empty and there weren't even any footprints. I returned inside, to check that nothing had been left behind, and it was then that I saw the writing on the wall.

Daylight shone into the cave, and I saw it clearly. Some of it had been graffitied with spray-cans and felt-tips, but some of it was older and had actually been engraved into the rock. I put my face up close and made out words that stretched off down the cave until they disappeared. '*We won't forget you*,' they said, and '*In respect*,' and '*Goodnight, God bless*,' and '*Your kind will never live again*.' Then there were dates that went back centuries, and I noticed that some of the messages were written in Welsh.

'*Ein tywysog olaf*,' one of them said. And '*Tywysog Cymru*,' said another.

And I mightn't know much Welsh, but – thanks to Grace – I knew what they meant.

Last Prince of Wales.

That's what they said – and then it all made sense. Of course it did, for I was Grace's grandson and I knew her stories, especially the one about the last real Prince of Wales, Llewellyn ap Gryffudd. I knew the castles that he'd built and the battles that he'd fought and I knew that, when he'd died, he took the hope of Wales with him. I also knew that his last night upon earth had been spent in some lonely cave, facing northwards into darkness.

Some lonely cave beside the Afon Gwy.

Suddenly I knew this was a place of pilgrimage. A shiver ran through me at the thought of Llewellyn's ghost sitting in the cave entrance, nursing his fire. Was that who he'd been? I've always liked to think he was, but he could have been just a pilgrim, taking refuge like me.

I read the names again, and would have added my own – sprayed my zed and dated it if I'd only had a can of paint. Instead I slipped away, glad that there were no signposts to this place or gift shops at its entrance. For what I took with me that day was far more valuable than any souvenir.

It was my life. I could have died that night, but here I was, no longer feeling like a dead weight, setting out renewed. I scrambled down the cliff, crossed the field beyond it and headed for the river. I could think straight again, and knew where I was going.

At last I reached the frozen river, which was covered with a fresh fall of snow. I ran to meet it, promising myself that, however bad things got, I'd never stray from it again but stay on course until I reached the sea. It was a wonderful reunion. I started downriver, full of new hope. I didn't even mind that I no longer had a sled and would have to make the journey on foot. Or so I thought until I got round the next bend and found Harri and Mari waiting for me!

They came bounding forward at the sight of me, pulling the sled after them. I could have wept, and hugged them half to death, scarcely able to believe that they had waited for me. It was a time for celebration. We ate a feast of Christmas leftovers before finally setting off, the three of us together again.

The miles fell behind us. I sat up on the high bench seat, wrapped against the cold with every blanket I could lay my hands on, and the tarpaulin thrown over the top. The sky was dull, and flecks of snow kept falling, but nothing could dampen my spirits. I even found myself singing.

We passed silent hills, thick with snow, and trees as tall and noble as cathedrals. Slowly but surely we were moving into a wild, remote region, far from human habitation. Pools stood deep and frozen, cataracts iced over in the act of tumbling into them. Forests stood stock-still, like soldiers at attention, and cliffs rose on either side of us, creating long, dark gorges that provided perfect spots for mounting ambushes and attacks.

This was border country, where wars had once been fought. Deep ravines forced the river into ever-narrowing channels. Somewhere along here, I knew, my grandmother's much-loved Afon Gwy would turn into the English River Wye. But nothing could dampen my spirits, not even leaving Wales behind, passing down its deepest, darkest gullies and waving them goodbye.

I was on my way to a new life, and nothing could stop me. No twist or turn in the river could put me off. Every obstacle was an opportunity waiting to be seized. Every boulder in the river, every fallen log, was one step closer to my destination.

I was certain that we'd reach the sea by nightfall. Only when the light began to fade did I realise that we'd have to spend another night out in the open. I looked at Harri and Mari and saw how tired they were, and felt ashamed of myself for having driven them so hard. We passed through the little English town of Hay-on-Wye, where we should have stopped to look for shelter, but the food was so low that we carried on.

A mile or so downriver, however, we could go no further. Even I could see that. We stopped in the shadow of a ruined castle where we ate a cold supper of bread and turkey scraps washed down with mouthfuls of snow. Then I released Harri and Mari from their harnesses and they bounded up and down the castle mound like children let out of school.

I followed at a more leisurely pace, climbing the mound in the hope of finding shelter at the top, only to discover that the castle was open to the elements. Not only that but, beyond its ruined walls, I couldn't see a place of shelter for miles. What were we going to do for the night?

I turned to leave, calling for Harri and Mari. But they totally ignored me, too busy digging holes in the snow to take any notice. It was as if their instincts for survival had taken over. When they'd formed a hole they liked, they flung themselves down into it, burrowing themselves as deeply as they could and then looking up at me, as if to say, 'There's room for three. What are you standing there for – *come and join us*.'

So I did. I mean, what else could I do? I got down in the hole with them, and let them press themselves against me as if to keep me warm. Their bodies stank to high heaven, but I was past caring. I pulled my coat round me and closed my eyes, not expecting to get to sleep, but it was surprisingly easy. The last thing I felt was snow falling on to my face, and the last thing I remember was the thought of tomorrow being better, because, if we survived the night, we'd hopefully reach the sea.

18

BEING HUNGRY

In the morning I discovered that the last of the food had gone. As if being half dead with the cold wasn't bad enough, we had been robbed! I made my way down to the sled to discover that our food boxes were empty and scattered over the ice. We had had visitors in the night. The last turkey scraps had gone and so had everything else, down to the last few crumbs of Pawl's Christmas cake.

Harri and Mari looked at me, as if to say, 'We didn't do it – it wasn't us,' and I looked at them as if to say, 'I didn't do it either.' I criss-crossed the ice, collecting empty boxes and lids, blaming myself for not having packed things away properly after we had eaten last night. There wasn't a single scrap of food left on the ice. All I could find were paw marks.

'Looks like foxes,' I said.

Harri and Mari looked at me as if to say they couldn't care less – all they cared about was that they were hungry. The bitter weather wasn't over yet and neither was our journey. What if we don't make it to the sea today? I thought. What are we going to do without food?

We set off downriver, with nothing for breakfast but handfuls of snow, and nothing to fall back on but an Extra Strong Mint that I found in Pawl's coat. I offered it to Harri and Mari but they turned up their noses and I ate it instead. Not that it made any difference – my stomach still felt empty.

One place followed another in dull succession. The sky was heavy with yet more snow, and a cold wind blew into our faces. I walked beside the sled, carrying as much as I could to try to lighten Harri and Mari's load. We came round a great bend in the river and, ahead of us, I caught sight of rooftops and spires. We were on the outskirts of Hereford. I recognised it immediately.

We passed under an old road bridge, and a rugby club came into view, followed by a sea cadet hut and a rowing club, another road bridge, made of concrete, and one made of stone. Then we found ourselves on a lovely stretch of river beyond which rose Hereford Cathedral – which I also recognised immediately, because I'd been dragged along to it a couple of times for concerts by my sister's school orchestra.

By now, we were close to the city centre. The bishop's palace stood on one side of us and a huge park on the other. The wind had dropped, and people had come out for fun. Suddenly ours wasn't the only sled on the river. We had joined the world of people again. Joined it with a vengeance! Skaters whizzed past and children threw snowballs. A hot dog stall stood parked on the riverbank and another, selling baked potatoes, had been wheeled out on to the ice.

I could smell food, and so could Harri and Mari. We stopped at a little jetty half-hidden from view by bushes and trees. 'You stay here,' I said to the dogs. 'Guard the sled while I go and find us something to eat.'

Looking back, I would have done better to let the dogs do their own foraging, but I tied up the sled and set off, promising Harri and Mari that I wouldn't be long. First I hung around the stalls hoping that somebody would drop their food, or put it down and forget it. But they didn't, and people began to stare as if there was something odd about me, so I headed off into the city centre instead, cutting through the gates that marked the boundary of the cathedral precinct and skirting round the edge of the green.

The cathedral loomed over me like an ocean liner in a sea of snow. A signpost offered a range of possibilities, from visiting the Mappa Mundi exhibition – dedicated to the cathedral's most famous treasure, a map of the medieval world – to buying snacks in the coffee shop. The cathedral was full of rich pickings, it suddenly occurred to me, and if I was lucky, they'd all be in the care of ancient colonels with wobbly legs and lavender-scented old ladies who couldn't see properly. There were the takings in all its tills, then there were collecting boxes for general upkeep, and golden crosses and candlesticks, and piles of silver plate, and even altar cloths embroidered with gold thread.

It'd be so easy, I thought. I could grab what I liked, sell it, and be set up for life. I'd never have to worry about food again!

But, in the end, I walked on. It was bad enough

being a murderer, I reckoned, without adding burglary to my crimes. Besides, knowing my luck, it wouldn't only be aged helpers who guarded the cathedral's treasures, but an army of hefty vicar-types who might wear frocks but looked as tough as rugby prop-forwards!

So I spent the afternoon scavenging through bins instead, though not with much success. Hereford, it seemed, wasn't a place where people threw away their food. Nor did they drop money. I scoured the icy pavements as well, but didn't find a single coin.

Finally, aware that people were staring again, I headed back across the cathedral precinct. I could tell what would happen if I stayed much longer. Hereford was like Pengwern – a world of Neighbourhood Watch and good citizenship, where everyone knew everyone else, and the police were always called at the first hint of anything suspicious.

By now, it was getting dark. Shops were closing and people starting to go home. A whole day had gone by. So much for telling the dogs that I wouldn't be long! Freezing cold, and feeling that I'd let them down badly, I somehow managed to miss the cathedral gates. Cursing myself for my mistake, I ended up in the cathedral garden enclosed by cloister walls. I should have turned back, but was so exhausted by this point that I decided to take a rest on one of the many benches facing the bushes in the centre of the garden.

No sooner had I sat down, though, than a group of boys came along. They scurried down the cloister dressed in long blue frocks and laughing to each other. For a moment I thought that they were laughing about me, but they disappeared through a side door into the cathedral without even looking my way. A little bit of light was briefly thrown across the garden, then the door shut behind them and darkness returned.

'*Is that the last of them? Have they gone?*' a voice said.

I looked around, but couldn't see a soul. 'Yes, they've gone,' I said.

'Good,' the voice said, and a boy appeared from behind a rubbish bin in the darkest corner of the cloister. He was probably my age, but very strangely dressed. Not only did he wear a long blue frock, just like the other boys, but over the top of it were layers of cloaks and capes embroidered in gold. He also wore golden shoes, and a tall gold hat decorated with what looked like strips of wallpaper cut into flame shapes.

Was the boy a weirdo? Or was he just going to a fancy-dress party? And if so, *what as?* Before I could ask him, he started throwing off his finery, revealing ordinary clothes underneath. He stuffed the golden clothes into the rubbish bin, produced a pair of trainers and started putting them on.

'If they come back looking for me, you won't tell?' he said, scarcely bothering to glance my way.

'What's it worth to you if I don't?' I answered, quick as a flash.

The boy shrugged. 'You can have this,' he said, digging a Mars bar out of his jacket pocket and throwing it my way.

I picked it up, wolfed it down and asked for more. 'That's surely not all you're offering,' I said. 'You must have something else. Money. Food. Anything will do.'

The boy stopped what he was doing and looked at

me, as if he'd caught the edge of desperation in my voice. I had made a big mistake. I turned my face away.

'Perhaps I *do* have something else,' he said, a hint of cunning in his voice. 'It all depends ...'

'Depends on what?' I said, again too quickly for my own good.

'It depends on *you*,' the boy said. 'There's a way that you could get all the money that you wanted, and the food. But you probably wouldn't want to. You wouldn't have the time, and you wouldn't be interested anyway. I mean, it's a bit of a bore. You've probably got better things to do with your time.'

He turned away as if he, too, had better things to do with his time. It was all a pretence, of course. He was desperate to catch me. And he did, as well!

'What's it all about?' I asked. 'What do I have to do?'

The boy grinned as if he'd got me, hook line and sinker. 'There's nothing to it,' he said. 'All you have to do is take my place in a little bit of pageantry in the cathedral. Dress up in my clothes, and march about. Every time you stop, the congregation will give you chocolate and cakes. And money, too. It's traditional, you see. A special Christmas custom. A bit of Christmas fun. I know it sounds crazy, but it's what they do.'

Now, of course, I know that it wasn't only crazy but a downright lie! And I probably knew it then, if I was honest with myself. But I was so desperate that I wouldn't listen to the warning voice inside. All I could think about was food and money – including a five-pound note that the boy found in his pocket and waved under my nose as a promise of what was to come.

'And all for a bit of walking about!' he said.

'What if someone realises that I'm not you?' I said.

'They won't,' he said. 'The cathedral's lit by candles for a do like this. Nobody can see a thing. Trust me.'

I allowed myself to be persuaded. My new chum gave me the fiver, and what had I got to lose? Quite a lot, as it turned out – but I didn't know that yet.

'*Oh, why not?*' I said, and made a grab for the funny clothes.

The boy helped me into them, plainly thrilled with the way things were turning out. I was a mate, he said – a sport, a great bloke, a gentleman and a chum. I said that he was a chum too. It was as if some strange insanity had taken hold of us. Together we pulled the blue frock over my head and smoothed it down over my trousers, put on the layers of cloaks and capes and got me into the golden shoes. Finally my new chum put the hat on to my head, ramming it down over my ears so that you could hardly see my face and telling me that it was called a mitre.

The name should have rung a warning bell but, for some strange reason, it didn't. Maybe I was too busy thinking about all the chocolate that I would soon be stuffing down, and the money in my pocket. Finally I was ready to go. The costume weighed a ton and looked ridiculous. It wasn't difficult to see why the boy had wanted to get out of wearing it. He tweaked it here and there, and pronounced me perfectly turned out.

'You'd better hurry. They'll be wondering where you are,' he said.

I felt my first surge of panic. 'All I have to do is

walk around?' I checked.

'That's right. Nothing to it,' my new chum said. 'Once they've marched you up and down, and given you the gold and grub, and sat you on the throne, that'll be the end of it – you can go home.'

The throne? *What throne?* Suddenly I realised that there were gaps in what the boy had told me. 'Wait a minute ...' I began.

Before I could say any more, however, the cathedral door burst open and two vicar-types bore down on me. 'There you are! Everybody's waiting. We're ready to get started,' they said.

What had I let myself in for? I felt another surge of panic and turned to tell the boy that I had changed my mind. But he wasn't there any more. He'd disappeared. I looked up and down the cloister, but couldn't see a soul. Apart from the vicar-types, of course.

'Let's be going, shall we?' they said, lining up on either side of me as if I were a prisoner and they my warders.

What was I going to do? I tried to come up with something, but it was already too late. They turned towards the door, and I knew that I was trapped. Then one of them saw something in the snow. He stooped and picked it up. At first I thought it was my fiver, fallen from my pocket, but then I saw that it was a piece of paper folded over several times.

The man glanced at it, then turned to me. 'For you,' he said, pressing it into my palm. 'You nearly forgot this, my lord bishop. You can't preach a sermon without your notes.'

19

THE BOY BISHOP

I entered the cathedral at the head of a procession of choirboys and candle-bearers, girls carrying golden crosses and black-frocked vicar-types. I didn't have a clue what was going on, but was too busy absorbing those two lethal phrases 'my lord bishop' and 'sermon notes' to do anything but keep on walking.

One thing was perfectly plain. *I had been tricked*. The piece of paper in my hand was a one-way ticket to some unknown hell.

What I should do, I thought, is get out quick – just like my new chum has obviously done!

By this time, however, it was too late. I was halfway down the cathedral, caught up in a drama that featured me in a starring role. Everybody peered at me as I passed by. I wondered if they realised that I was the wrong boy. Every time I stopped for my gifts of chocolate, cakes and money, the girls with golden crosses nudged me on, rolling their eyes as if they didn't know what was the matter with me.

By the time I reached the bottom end of the

cathedral I knew there were no gifts, and that I'd been tricked in this as well. As the great west doors drew close, I prepared to run away. Before I could, however, the organ boomed into life, and the choirboys erupted with a sound that gave a whole new meaning to the words *Christmas carol.*

I felt it behind me like a cannon going off. My hair stood up on end, and the sheer volume of sound propelled me forward like a tank leading a charge. It was a wonderful moment. Suddenly I felt powerful and excited, caught up in something that was bigger than all my fears put together. The next thing I knew, I was halfway up the central aisle, belting out the carol with the rest of the choirboys, not caring how tuneless and untrained I must have sounded beside their perfect pitch. Just for a moment, I felt as if I could take on the world.

But then the moment ended. The high altar appeared ahead of me, carved in stone, lit by candles and decorated with gold. Above it hung a massive, stained-glass windowpane depicting God in aquamarine robes. His all-seeing face looked down at me as if he'd know the wrong boy anywhere, regardless of the candlelight. I blushed as if caught out, and my voice dried up. No longer did I feel like a battle tank leading a charge. Instead I felt like an enemy spy trying to sneak in under cover of darkness.

The choristers peeled away on either side of me, taking their places in the choir stalls, leaving me alone. I stood before a carved throne, its candles lighting up a man in a purple robe.

The choristers stopped singing, and the man stood up. In his hand he held a staff, curved at the top to look like a golden question mark. I realised that he was the bishop – the real bishop, I mean, not the '*my lord bishop*' that the vicar-type had jokingly called me. He looked at me, and I looked back. An absolute stillness fell across the cathedral as if something very special was about to happen.

Then the man came down from the throne, removed the plain gold cross that hung round his neck, and hung it round mine. He took the ring off his finger and put it on mine, and handed me the golden staff. Finally I stood before him, covered in the sort of treasure that only hours earlier I'd imagined stealing.

'*Except ye be made like unto little children,*' he cried out in a great voice, standing before the congregation, stripped bare of all his symbols of office, '*ye shall not enter the Kingdom of Heaven! On this great Feast of Holy Innocents – BEHOLD OUR BISHOP OF THE INNOCENTS!*'

Suddenly it was like a charge going off. A wave of feeling ran around the cathedral. For everybody else, I realised, this was a holy moment, but for me it couldn't possibly have been worse. Bishop of what? *The Innocents?* Was that what the man had said? I broke out in a sweat. Surely he hadn't been referring to me? He couldn't have done. Not possibly.

Not the murderer of Gilda Katterfelto!

I should have turned tail, right there and then, and got out. Before I could do anything, however, the bishop spun me round to face the congregation too. I stood before them all, waiting for God to strike me dead. I was shaking from head to foot, and everybody could see it. The bishop patted my shoulders, as if to say that all boys got nervous at this point, and I wasn't to worry.

'*They shall put down the mighty from their seats,*' he cried out in his great, booming voice. '*And exalt the humble and meek.*'

Then he took me firmly by the elbows and sat me on the throne between the candles. The choirboys burst into an anthem and the organ thundered so loudly that the whole cathedral trembled. I waited to die, thinking that if I'd been God I'd have finished me off ages ago, before I'd even dared enter the cathedral.

But the anthem finished and nothing happened except that the eyes of the congregation turned back to me. The bishop offered up a prayer for the 'sweet-smelling savour of a life of innocence'. Then he made a holy sign in the air and the girls with golden crosses got on either side of me.

I was off on my travels again. With the girls in front of me and the bishop bringing up the rear, we processed between the choir stalls, heading for the pulpit. We reached its steps, and I looked up with dread. Behind me I could hear the bishop whispering that I'd be all right so long as I remembered to 'speak clearly and *project your voice*.'

I had no choice. I climbed the steps, thinking that if God hadn't struck me yet, he would now. The congregation stared up at me – all the great and good of Hereford, including the mayor and mayoress in their chains of office. And I stared back, knowing that I was a black sheep in their midst and that, however many rivers I travelled down, or golden robes I hid behind, I could never escape from what I'd done.

I hung my head. Somewhere below the pulpit, I heard the bishop clear his throat. I could feel him willing me to do well. And I might be a black sheep, but I still had a sermon to preach!

Remembering the piece of paper in my hand, I opened it out. At the top, promisingly enough, was written the heading, 'Boy Bishop's Sermon – Feast of Holy Innocents'. But underneath it were four words.

I can't! OH SHIT!!

That was it. Nothing else. I stared at the blank page, knowing that, when I found my so-called chum – *and I would* – another murder would take place! The congregation looked up at me, their expressions freezing over with embarrassment as it dawned on them that I had dried up. The bishop cleared his throat again, trying to gently prod me into action, and the vicar-types glanced at each other as if only now were they realising that something was amiss. The choirmaster looked fully into my face and visibly flinched, and the choristers all grinned, as if they'd realised from the start – and thought the whole thing a great joke.

The game was up. I did the only thing possible in the circumstances – leapt down from the pulpit and legged it out of the cathedral. As I went, I flung off the layers of golden clothing, telling myself that I might be a black sheep but at least I wasn't a thief. The congregation watched in astonishment, as mitre, ring, staff, golden cross, golden cloaks and capes and golden shoes flew in every direction. I reached the great west doors of the cathedral, pulled them open and dashed outside.

It was the last that any of them saw of me. I ran

barefooted across the snowy precinct, not even noticing how cold it was. I didn't know where I was going and didn't care either. All I knew was that I'd got to get away.

I left the precinct behind, and ran around the city centre like a crazy thing. People must have stared at me, but I didn't notice. Gradually I got colder until finally I had no choice but to return to the cloister garden. Here I dug my coat and boots out of the rubbish bin. The cathedral lights were out by now, and its precinct had fallen silent. The great and good of Hereford had all gone home and the place was deserted. My so-called chum had gone as well, which came as no surprise, but he'd left a note on the bench where I'd been sitting, which said, 'Thanks a bunch.'

I screwed it up, and was just about to throw it in the bin when the cathedral side door opened and footsteps came my way. A couple of vicar-types appeared, locked in conversation about the calibre of boy you got these days in choir schools. They hadn't seen me yet but, knowing that they soon would, I crept into the shadows, looking for a hiding place.

This I found, much to my surprise, in the cathedral coffee shop, whose door I discovered had been left unlocked. I hid behind it until the vicar-types had gone, then, as I turned to leave, I noticed a light next door, in the room that housed the famous Mappa Mundi.

Had somebody stolen it, or was it simply that the person responsible for security round here had taken leave of their senses that night? I went to check, and found the map still hanging on the wall. I'd seen it once before, dragged here by my parents after one of

Cary's concerts, but had been so impatient to get away that I'd hardly bothered to look at it.

Now I stood before it again, with all the time in the world, noticing how different it was to an ordinary map. For starters, everything was in the wrong place according to the ordinary rules of geography. Then some of the places were real, while others were places I'd only ever thought of as existing in myth. Then there were people on the map – kings and saints and people like that. Then there were creatures too, and some of them were real live creatures that you saw in zoos, but others – like the griffin and the unicorn – were out of myths as well.

But there they hung, on the wall, as if the map was big enough for all of them. And I thought about that afterwards, miles downriver in the dark with the wind whistling through the trees.

I wish I had a map like that, I thought, with everything on it – all the places that I've been to, and the things I've seen, all the people, and the creatures, and Plynlimon and the sea. Then when I'm feeling frightened, like I do now, I'll at least know I belong, and where I might end up.

20

SEVEN SISTERS' ROCKS

I returned to Harri and Mari bearing a pocket full of burgers bought with my five-pound note. I was overwhelmed with guilt for having been away for so long, but they leapt all over me as if they bore no grudge. We divided the burgers between us and wolfed them down. Then we set off again.

I was glad to see the lights of Hereford disappearing. For evermore, I'd remember it as the place where I'd learnt that I couldn't run away from what I'd done to Gilda. I sat up on the high bench seat, wondering with dread what my journey would teach me next. I tried to comfort myself with the thought of my seafaring father waiting for me when I got to the sea. But, in my new state of clear-sightedness, I knew that I was kidding myself.

We rested in a barn but I couldn't sleep. At first light we set off again, but the only thing that kept me going was the promise I'd made after my night in Llewellyn's cave not to give up. There seemed no point to anything any more. I huddled on the bench seat, watching Harri and Mari pulling the sled, and wishing I had half their spirit.

All that day I felt edgy and nervous. Time and time again, I found myself glancing back, as if the whistling of the wind meant that the *Cŵn y Wbir* were after me. There wasn't anything to see, but maybe Harri and Mari started sensing something too, because they began to falter.

For the first time in our journey, they began to look as if they didn't want to carry on. The wind was bitter and gusty, buffeting against them, and I had to shout to keep them going. I felt ashamed, but also felt as if I had no choice. There was snow in the wind – hard, pitted white stuff that stung my face and stuck like glue. Soon my body was covered with it, and so were the dogs' coats.

We passed snowed-in villages where houses were covered too, and cars buried in their drives. Electric lines were down, candles shone in windows, and not a soul was about. Then we passed through open country where the wind created massive drifts. It was difficult to keep going. Snow piled up on the sled until it felt as if it weighed a ton.

Harri and Mari became slower and slower and, finally, I had to call a halt. I didn't want to, but knew that I had no choice. I unharnessed the dogs and they stood looking up at me, too tired even to shake the snow off their coats. Once they'd flown like wild creatures set free, but now they stood like beasts of burden, wretched and exhausted.

'This can't go on,' I said. '*We* can't go on. You've got to head back home. Go back to Pawl. I know that you can find him. I never should have brought you. You're better off without me. Off with you – go, go, *go*!'

I waved my arms like windmills, trying to shoo Harri and Mari away. But instead of seizing their chances, they stood in front of me refusing to budge. I tried again, shouting in a loud, rough voice that I'd had enough of them and trying to push them away. But they continued to look up at me.

In the end, there was no choice but for us to carry on. We sheltered for a while behind a hedge, then started off again. The journey was no easier – the snow still fell, the cold was still cold and the wind still blew mercilessly. But everything felt different. If the whole world turned its back on me, I knew I'd still have Harri and Mari. At least I wouldn't be alone.

It was a good feeling. But feelings don't fill stomachs and, all too soon, mine was rumbling miserably. The previous night's burgers felt as if they'd happened years ago. We passed a riverside pub called The Hope & Anchor, and I remember thinking that there was precious little hope on our journey any more, and absolutely nothing to anchor us.

The rest of the day passed in a blur of hungriness and confusion. Daylight seeped away – not that there had ever been much of it, anyway. We passed beneath an old stone bridge, and started down a valley in the shadow of yet another ruined castle. The riverbank closed in on either side of us. Trees hung over the frozen water, and I noticed berries hanging from them. Bright red berries standing out against a tangle of dark branches – and I don't know what got into me, but suddenly I found myself picking them.

If not the worst mistake of my whole life, it wasn't far off. I did it out of desperation, I suppose, because I had no food and it was cold and dark. And, once I'd started eating, I couldn't stop. I stuffed them all down – hard little berries and softer ones, bitter ones and a few that were mercifully tasteless. Some I chewed and some I swallowed whole.

It was madness, of course. I mean, they didn't even satisfy my hunger. But I kept on stuffing them down, telling myself that of course they weren't poisonous, and the countryside was full of food for free if only people had the guts to eat the stuff. Finally, when I could take no more, I washed the last berries down with a handful of snow. And who can say which did most harm in the end? Perhaps the softer ones were as poisonous as the hard ones.

Certainly it didn't take me long to find out. By now the journey had drawn us into a deep gorge with densely wooded cliffs on either side. The river looped around these cliffs, turning first one way and then the other, and I began to get queasy feelings, as if I was on a fairground ride.

At first I blamed the dogs for pulling the sled roughly, making it swing from side to side. The alternative – that the berries were to blame – was too terrible to contemplate. But then my stomach started churning in a truly alarming fashion, and I knew that I was in serious trouble. Sweat broke out all over me and the churning turned into waves of violent stomach cramps. Nausea washed over me, and I knew it was all down to the berries.

'*No*,' I said. 'I'm imagining it. I've got to pull myself together. There's nothing wrong with me.'

But the words were scarcely out before I found myself hanging over the side of the sled, watching the contents of my stomach shooting out all over the ice. I had never been so sick in my life. Harri and Mari stopped and looked at me, plainly unsure what to do. My stomach cramps got worse and I crawled off across the ice to relieve myself. This was a cruel and lengthy business, best left undescribed, if not forgotten. After it was over, I lay where I was and wanted to die. The world was going round in circles, and wouldn't stop. I was shaking with the cold, and with fear as well. I'd had stomach upsets before, but never anything like this!

Somehow, I struggled back to the sled and we started off again. It was a nightmare journey, which seemed to have no end. The gorge closed in on either side with huge, forbidding cliffs hanging over me. I clung to the sides of the sled and wondered how long I could possibly survive.

A village came into view, snow-bound and silent. I saw lights on a cliff top, a pub with a car park, a riverside hotel and a row of ferries trapped in the ice. Then, all too quickly, the village was gone again, replaced by a dark stretch of river where there wasn't a hint of light. Trees lined empty ridges, pointing skywards in rows like quivers full of arrows. Mist clung to the trees, and it felt like a place of ghosts. A place of slaughter, terrible and silent. I couldn't get away from it quickly enough.

Perhaps Harri and Mari felt the same, because they suddenly started running. I don't know where they got their energy from, but they tore down the gorge as if the hounds of hell were after them. I swung from side to side of the sled, unable to control them. Could anything be worse than this? I thought.

My stomach lurched again, and I broke out in another sweat. Something was wrong with me – and it wasn't just the berries. Breathing in, I felt a ring of iron tighten round my chest and, breathing out, I dissolved into coughs. Not only that, but my throat and ears had started burning and my limbs throbbed. My body felt as weak and helpless as a newborn baby's. Sweat began to pour off me, and it was obvious that I had caught a fever.

The sled passed underneath a wooden footbridge and made its way round another great loop in the river. The black cliffs fell behind me and new ones loomed ahead, covered in trees with huge white rocks sticking out of them like a row of skulls. I moved towards them, feeling like a mariner in uncharted waters. My whole body was aching fit to burst.

Suddenly the moon came out from behind a cloud. It lit the gorge, chasing away the darkness. The river shone as if made of silver, and the white rocks shone as if somebody had switched on a light. I counted them as I passed underneath. Numbered each of them, and they came to seven.

And, when I saw the girls beneath them, skating on the ice, there were seven of them too.

21

ICEBREAK

The skaters shone like silver in the moonlight, dancing in circles and all holding hands. At first they looked like elves caught up in magic rituals but, as the sled moved towards them, I saw coats, jackets, bags and boots thrown all over the riverbank as if they weren't fairy folk after all, but a modern sisterhood complete with all its fashion accessories.

I also saw a big camp fire and the remains of a fry-up which spilled out of silver-foil packages and billy-cans. Sausages. Bacon. Fried bread. Baked beans. Even baked potatoes. Harri and Mari headed towards them but, as soon as I was close enough to catch a whiff, my stomach heaved and I was sick.

This stopped the girls in their tracks. They turned and stared at us and one of them, taller and older-looking than the rest, broke ranks and skated over. She was dressed in white, her hair bobbed behind her in a golden ponytail and everything about her shone. She could have been a silver screen goddess caught by paparazzi cameras instead of just some girl lit by the full moon.

'Are you all right?' she said. 'What are you doing out here on the ice? Don't you have anyone to look after you?'

I stared at her weakly, unable to speak. The girl took my hand, then felt my forehead. 'You're burning up,' she said. 'You've got a raging temperature. I don't know what you think you're doing, but you must be mad. On a night like this, you should be home in bed!'

This was hardly calculated to make me feel better but, strangely, it did. The girl called the others over, and they got me off the sled and half-dragged, half-carried me to the fire. The first girl was definitely the one in charge. I listened to her telling the other what to do as if she was their bossy eldest sister.

'That's right,' she said. 'Have you got him? Look out, his boots are slipping off! They're not tied properly. Bring him this way – yes, that's it! Be careful, you two at the back – don't drop him! Yes, that's right, gently, gently, down here by the fire ...'

I smelt it before I even got to it – smelt its warm, sweet savour and felt safe. The girls lay me down beside it, with a pillow of scarves under my head and their coats piled over me. Some of them went back to unharness Harri and Mari. They brought them to the fire too, and I remember dimly thinking that they deserved all the fuss and attention that they were getting.

Then I must have dropped off to sleep because, the next thing I knew, Harri and Mari were forgotten and the girls were round me again. In the moonlight, every single one of them looked like a silver screen goddess. I could scarcely believe that they were real.

'You're in good hands,' the first girl said, touching

my cheek as if to prove how real she was. 'Everything's all right. Don't you worry. You're safe with us.'

I didn't doubt that I was. But *safe* was one thing and *better* was another, and one minute I was freezing and the next I was sweating. I couldn't stop coughing, couldn't stop being sick, and the seven girls clustered round me might be goddesses but they certainly weren't doctors!

Not that that seemed to bother them. With quiet efficiency, they set to work. The first girl stayed to hold me upright while I was sick, and lay me down again afterwards, while the others hurried about, building up the fire and collecting ice off the river. I'd no idea what they were up to, but they filled a billy-can, put it on the fire and waited for the ice to melt. Then, when it was boiling hard, they took it off the fire and stuck it in the snow to cool down.

Finally, when it was cool enough, they brought it to the first girl, who sat me up and put it in my hands. I looked into the billy-can and saw a scummy mess of river water with bits of leaves and twigs and goodness knows what else floating on its surface. It wasn't very appetising, to put it mildly.

'I know it may seem crazy,' the first girl said. 'But we know what we're doing. Honestly. Trust us.'

I did, too. Trust them, I mean. Goodness knows why, but when the billy-can was put to my lips, I decided to take the risk. Its contents might look like the most unlikely medicine I'd ever seen, but I took a sip – and the drink tasted fine. Surprisingly fine. In fact, it actually tasted a bit like wine!

I took another sip, thinking that it tasted even more

like wine – and a decent wine as well. Then my head started spinning and I went back for a third sip. And then I took a fourth, and my head began to spin even more.

All too quickly the billy-can emptied. The girls looked down at me, their faces wreathed in smiles. I started feeling sleepy and they blurred in and out of vision. The first girl said something to me, but her voice seemed to come from far away.

She lay me down again, and covered me with coats and the tarpaulin off the sled. By now I could scarcely keep my eyes open. The girls seemed miles away, and years away as well, fading from the present as if the past was taking them and leaving me behind.

I closed my eyes. '*Now go to sleep*,' I heard the first girl whispering. '*Let the river work its magic.*'

In the morning, I woke up cured. I knew it even before I opened my eyes. Knew that I was strong again, and restored in every way. I didn't feel weak after being so sick. I wasn't coughing any more and wasn't in a sweat. The band of iron had gone from round my chest, and I didn't ache any more.

Instead I felt ready for the new day. I got up. The camp fire had burned out and the coats had gone, along with every other trace of the seven sisters. But the blankets off the sled had been tucked tightly round my body, with the tarpaulin laid over them to keep me dry. Harri and Mari got up too. They shook themselves and we set off again. They were restored as well, their eyes bright and their heads up as they pulled the sled downriver.

It was a wonderful morning. I sat on the high bench seat, convinced that this would be the day when we finally made it to the sea. I looked for it round every twist and turn in the gorge and I even sang, if I remember rightly. I couldn't see a snow cloud anywhere, and the air actually had a bit of warmth to it for a change. My mind ran on ahead of me to the river estuary where, as if my faith in the impossible had been restored, I could picture my seafaring father waiting for me.

The dogs strained forward, as if they had dreams of their own. Poor Harri and Mari – I can see them still, the sun above them and their feet flying down the icy river. They had no idea what lay ahead, and neither did I.

We came bursting out of the gorge, glad to be alive, to find that every branch on every tree was hung with diamond drops of water caught by the sun. They sparkled in the soft air, and I should have added two and two together and recognised a thaw when I saw one.

Before I could do anything, however, a sudden cracking sound had me jumping out of my skin. It sounded like a gun going off – a shooter in a wood, or something like that. Harri and Mari flinched, but I'm certain they would have carried on if there hadn't been a second crack, even louder than the first, and closer too.

They reared up in confusion, and I struggled to calm them down. But then we heard a third crack, even closer still, and they spun round on the ice and I lost control. For a moment I was almost tipped out of the sled, then it righted itself and Harri and Mari went bolting back the way we'd come, dragging me behind them, clinging to the sled to stay onboard.

There was nothing I could do to stop them. The gorge's shadows fell across us, and we bumped and lurched, twisted and turned our way past everything I'd thought we'd said goodbye to. Finally we found ourselves back in the dark place again, where the ridges of trees looked like quivers full of arrows.

The place I'd thought of as a place of slaughter.

I'll never forget it. Ahead of us, I could see the village with the hotel and the ice-locked ferries. But, before we could reach it, another shot rang out. It sounded right behind us this time, and I spun round to find a black snake racing up the ice towards us.

A long, black, twisting, turning *snake*!

I cried out in a panic, unable to understand quite what was going on. And after that it's hard to put anything in order. It happened so very quickly. I remember the dogs rearing up. I remember the way the river shook as the snake passed by. I remember the sled being struck, and the snake running under it like black lightning, and then carrying on upriver. I remember it reaching the village and the ferries bobbing up and down.

But it was only when I saw the water rising up like black blood all around me, that anything made sense. It came bursting out of the snake and, suddenly, I understood. The sunny day, the dripping trees, the spring-like weather – of course. *This was a thaw!*

Suddenly there wasn't just the one snake on the river. There were hundreds of them running about in every direction. As far back as the footbridge, I could see – and hear – the frozen river breaking into pieces. And I could see it ahead too: the ferries at the hotel careering round like fairground rides, and a network of chasms opening up around them.

Everywhere I looked, the river was rising up. Only last night it had saved me, but now it felt like an enemy. I couldn't believe that it was the same river. The power that the thaw had unleashed made it unrecognisable.

I tried to get away, steering the sled across what remained of the ice. But it was impossible to stay upright, let alone escape. Water slopped over me as I tried to right the sled, and over Harri and Mari too, as they tried to help. We did our best, aiming for the shore, but the river was impossible to navigate.

When a chasm opened up beneath us, there was nothing we could do. The sled went one way, me clinging on to it, and Harri and Mari went the other. All that connected us were ropes and harnesses. I struggled to pull them back, and the dogs struggled to reach my outstretched hands. They nearly did it, too, but suddenly a pair of massive ice floes crashed between us like heavy-duty pincers, cutting through everything that bound us together and sending Harri and Mari down through the black water.

I couldn't save them.

All that I could do was watch it happening.

It was over very quickly. One minute Harri and Mari were flailing about in the freezing water, and then they were gone and I had no time to mourn them because I was nearly gone myself. I was still clinging on to the sled – goodness only knows how – but the river rose to greet me and I slipped beneath its surface. I could feel the sled pulling me down, and realised that, if I didn't let go, I would sink with it.

And so I did. Let go, I mean. I let the sled slip away

from me, and sink without a trace. My grandmother's red wicker sled, inherited by Pawl along with Harri and Mari. I never saw it again, and I never saw them either. All that was left was a broken plank from the high bench seat, which I found bobbing on the water and grabbed for dear life.

It must have been what saved me. I've no memory at all of how I got out of the river – just a dim recollection of black figures running up and down the hotel car park in the distance. One minute I was treading water, wondering what had happened to my boots and surrounded by ice floes. Then darkness fell, and the one clear thing I do remember is swearing that, if I survived, I would never swim again.

And ever afterwards I've always hated water. It took me years to break that vow. Years to swim again, and even then I hated it. And this is why.

22

THE SPEECH HOUSE HOTEL

What happened that day changed me. Ever since, in small ways and large, I've been different. Something died in me when the dogs went down, but something else was born. No longer did I look for happy endings as if I stood a chance of finding them, or believe in the power of my imagination to make my dreams come true.

But a new determination came over me. Life was a battle for survival – and one that I would win! I've been a fool, I thought. A stupid fool on a stupid journey, going nowhere and not even knowing it. And now, because of me, Harri and Mari are dead.

I became tougher after that. Sharper, and less squeamish about things like right and wrong. Take stealing, for example. Once I'd break out in a sweat at the thought of doing anything like that. But now something dogged and determined got hold of me. The thing that mattered most was staying alive. And I'd do whatever it took. Take whatever I found. Find what I needed and stay alive at all costs!

'Nothing in the world,' I told myself, 'not hunger, cold, exhaustion or some trifling matter of who owns what, is going to get in my way!'

My first theft took place in the village, up the road from the hotel. A house stood on its own, without lights and surrounded by trees. I walked straight in, dripping all over the floor, grabbed a handful of clothes off a drying rack, stuffed them into a bin bag and walked out again. Nobody saw me. Maybe the owners of the house were down by the river watching the pantomime on the ice.

I even helped myself to a fridge full of cold meats and a camouflage jacket hanging on the back door. Then I did the same at the next house that I came to, only to find that I couldn't get beyond the conservatory and would have to make do with a pair of gardening boots tied up with string.

It wasn't much but, in the forest afterwards, changing into dry clothes, I told myself it was enough. I left behind my old clothes, buried in the snow, but hung on to Pawl's coat even though it was too wet to wear, stuffing it into the empty bin bag because it was all that I had left of my old life. Then I started through the forest, climbing up the gorge without a clue where I was heading, but thinking that anywhere would do, just as long as it was out of here.

I didn't like this dripping gorge. The snow was disappearing fast, and the ground beneath it was boggy and grey. Streams of melted snow ran everywhere and the trees hung sadly, as if the carnival was over. I knew I'd never have another journey like the one I'd just had with Harri and Mari. Everything was ordinary again. Everything was disappointing.

I reached the top of the gorge at last, and the river lay beneath me. For a moment I stood watching it twisting and turning out of sight, then I turned away. I walked all that day without knowing where I was going. Ahead of me lay a sodden, never-ending forest where everything seemed dead. If the sun shone, it was always high up among the treetops, never reaching the forest floor. Even when it sank, it didn't reach the forest floor, just faded slowly somewhere off between the trees until there wasn't anything left to lighten my path.

I was in deep forest, lost in the night. Once or twice I heard cars in the distance, but I never saw any headlights or came across a road. Gradually my eyes grew accustomed to the dark, and I made out forest paths and old abandoned railway tracks, which I followed for miles. I passed deep streams, buried in banks of peat, and ponds that would have been frozen over only hours ago, but now they rippled in the evening breeze.

Later that night, I hit a road with houses on it, and streetlights. It was the outskirts of a town. I passed along its pavements, picking food out of bins. Nobody was about, streets empty and pubs closed. But curtains twitched as I walked by, and a couple of cars slowed down so that their drivers could take a second look, checking on this foreigner in their town.

It was a relief to reach the other side, and return into the forest. Its huge old trees threw their shadows over me and I walked freely again without fear of being observed. I was shattered by this time, but had worked myself into a frame of mind where stopping was unthinkable.

'I'll carry on for ever,' I told myself. 'Nothing's

going to stop me. Even if I found the sea, I'd carry on until its waves broke over me. And then I'd carry on. I'd never stop. I'd walk for ever and never give up.'

It was crazy, of course. In the end, of course, I *had* to stop. Somewhere in the darkness, my body said enough's enough. I don't remember where it was, or what exactly happened, but I woke up in the morning to find myself lying under a huge old sump in an oily-smelling corrugated hut. This, I discovered when I staggered outside, was part of an abandoned coal-mine, overgrown with moss and bracken. Piles of slag lay outside the hut. Bits of broken railway track disappeared into the forest and I even found a couple of chipped coffee mugs sitting on a tree trunk as if the miners might come back.

Perhaps this mine wasn't as abandoned as I'd first thought. It didn't look very likely, but I hurried off just in case, my legs like rusty pistons cranking into action. I didn't have a clue where I was going or what would happen next, but I didn't care. The thing that mattered was the doing. The getting up again. The going through the motions.

I walked for hours, just like the day before. Mostly the forest was silent, but occasionally birds cried out warnings as I approached, or a little breeze got up and whispered through the trees. A couple of times I passed houses where I sneaked in and grabbed food.

Once I even climbed up to a viewing point where I could see the forest stretching away to the horizon. There would be roads beneath those trees, and towns and villages too, but I couldn't see them. I couldn't see a single sign of life.

It was a gloomy prospect. I set off again, wandering

aimlessly for hours and ending up in a vast boggy region where all the melted snow in the forest, it seemed, had drained into a natural sink. A network of peat ditches lay beneath my feet. I tried to keep out of them, looking for higher ground, but the boggy region stretched on and on. Brambles caught me in their branches, and huge old holly trees pressed in on every side. I sank up to my ankles and even left my boots behind and had to dig them out.

Finally the forest fell silent and the sun began to sink. Soon it would be dark again, and I'd be stuck here for another night. I forced myself on, but the going got no better. I couldn't even see where I was putting my feet any more and, to make matters worse, a little bit of mist was beginning to drift my way.

I veered away from it instinctively, and it was then that I started hearing things. To begin with the sounds were too far off to care about but, as I edged away from the mist, it seemed to me that they grew. Then I started seeing things as well – little bits of light that came and went like waves on a moonlit sea. And the sounds were like the sea too. They drifted towards me and faded away like waves washing over pebbles.

I forced myself forward, hope springing to life again against all odds. What if, despite everything, I'd reached my journey's end? *What if the sea lay ahead of me?* The ground became drier and the trees thinned out. I made my way between them, my heart pounding. But it wasn't the sea that I found waiting for me when I stepped out from between the trees. It was a road.

It stretched before me, bright with headlights making their way home. I had got it wrong about the waves and pebbles. What I'd heard were tyres on wet tarmac, cutting through the forest at high speed. I stood watching cars disappearing one after another, cross with myself for expecting anything else. Finally nothing else came along and the road emptied.

Then I stepped on to it, and started walking. It was a long road, and perfectly straight, stretching away in either direction for as far as I could see. Trees grew right up to the edge of it and their darkness pressed in around me. In the distance I could see a solitary light, but I didn't take much notice until I drew level with it and saw that it was an illuminated road sign advertising hotel accommodation.

THE SPEECH HOUSE HOTEL
AA THREE-STAR RATED
FOUR-POSTER BEDROOMS AVAILABLE
OLD FOREST OF DEAN HOSTELRY
ESTABLISHED 1676

I couldn't actually see a hotel, but a short walk further down the road brought into view a fine old country house, its tall chimneys standing against the night sky. Tiled across its entrance porch was the word WELCOME, and through its leaded windows I could see guests moving about from one bar to another, carrying drinks. They were all dressed up, the men in black bow ties and the ladies in cocktail dresses, as if for a grand gala occasion. I wondered what they were celebrating until I noticed a banner in the reception area wishing everybody a HAPPY NEW YEAR.

This came as a surprise. Christmas was hardly over in my mind, and now it seemed that the year was almost over too, and a new one on its way. Where had all the time gone? I stood staring at the banner, feeling strangely confused. A car came along the road, and I had to step out of the way. When it had gone, I noticed a gathering of mist down in a dip. Then a ripple of breeze came running up the road from nowhere in particular. It caught my hair and carried on through the forest. Trees murmured to each other and I saw their topmost branches swaying.

I found myself shivering. I looked along the road again, and it seemed to me that the mist was growing. It was getting longer, and thicker too, forming itself into white fingers that almost looked as if they were reaching out for me. There was something in the mist too – something stealthy and moving my way.

'What's going on?' I whispered.

Almost as if in answer, something flew overhead. Where it came from I'd no idea, but it cried out as it flew away, and brushed my hair, and suddenly I felt as if I was back on Plynlimon with some crabbing crow flying over me. I spun round, only to discover that the mist was there as well. It had crept up behind me. The forest was full of it.

'No!' I cried. But yes, the mist was there – and suddenly I felt as if everything I'd ever done had led me to this moment. Not just the long miles of my journey, but everything else. Don't ask me why, but that's how I felt. Back it all went, even past my fateful bet with Cary. It was as if this lonely spot, buried in the heart of the forest, was where everything, finally, caught up with me. And what could I do to save myself? Where could I hide?

There was only one answer.

The Speech House Hotel.

23

THE RED JUDGE

I entered the hotel, closing both outer and inner porch doors behind me, as if afraid that the mist would follow me in. The reception area was empty, much to my relief. Only moments ago it had been full, but now nobody lounged in its sinking sofas or basked around its huge fire. Even the main desk was empty, and the only voices that I heard came from the inner office.

I had chosen the right moment. I hurried past the reception desk before anyone returned, and slipped into the interior corridors of the hotel. I was looking for a door to lock behind me – somewhere deep and dark where I could hide until the mist had gone. But every door I came to either had voices behind it or was locked already. It was the same upstairs too. I hurried up to the first floor landing, but couldn't even find an unlocked cupboard.

Only when I climbed another set of stairs, and ended up on the second floor, did I find a door that opened. It led into a guest bedroom that had obviously been taken for the night, but I didn't mind because its occupants were elsewhere. I locked it behind me, crept into their bathroom, locked that door as well and prayed that they wouldn't return. Then – seasoned veteran of horror movies that I was – I blocked the plugholes in the bath and hand basin, put down the toilet seat, shut the ventilation grille and even lay a wet towel under the door so that nothing, especially fingers of white mist, could get in.

I felt pretty stupid doing it, but not so stupid that I didn't bother. I got into the shower, pulled the curtain round me and stood shaking all over. I was safe, I told myself, but I couldn't stop. In fact, I was still doing it when the occupants of the room returned.

I heard their key turn in the lock, then they came hurrying in, passing the bathroom and going on at each other about being late. Lights went on, metal hangers clanged in the wardrobe and I caught snatches of conversation about dresses and cufflinks and clip-on bow ties.

Any minute now, I thought, and they're going to want the bathroom.

I waited for it, braced for trouble but, after a while, everything fell quiet. Deciding that the couple must have left again, I opened the bathroom door to check. This was a mistake as they hadn't gone anywhere but stood before the window, staring at the forest as if they'd forgotten they were late.

And who could blame them? Beyond the window, the sky was lit up by a huge moon, but the forest floor was full of mist. It wove intricate patterns between the trees, creating shapes that kept on shifting and regrouping. I'd never seen mist do that before – never seen it move so fast. The moon shone down on it, making the forest glow like those aerial shots of night-time cities where the movement has been speeded up. But its light was cold. There was no warmth to it. For all its movement, it had no life.

I turned back to the bathroom, but the couple heard me. They spun round and saw what must have looked to them like a murderous thug, bent on stealing their belongings. They cried out in alarm, and I tore off, knowing that if they caught me I was done for. I raced along the landing with them in pursuit, down the stairs, through a set of fire doors and down yet more stairs, finally reaching the ground floor.

Here I pushed my way past waiters who were gliding in and out of the dining room, beneath a massive WELCOME banner, serving dinner to their gala guests. Most of them got out of my way, but one crashed into me and, in the general commotion of cursing hotel staff and irate guests, I shot off down another set of stairs, which led into the basement.

Here I shut the first door that I reached behind me, and took the precaution of turning the key. Immediately I felt as if I'd stepped into another world. The air was cold and still and musty, but it was wonderfully quiet and I knew no one would find me.

This is more like it, I thought, creeping through the darkness looking for a place to hide. But, every step I took, the basement seemed to get colder. It was as if it had been refrigerated. I began to wonder if I'd got myself into more trouble than if I'd stayed upstairs. But then I came to a door with a light shining under it, and I pushed it open – and found myself in another dining room.

Like the one upstairs, it had been prepared as if for

a grand gala occasion, tables laid with cloths and candlesticks and crystal glasses. In fact, I almost thought it *was* the dining room upstairs, and that I'd somehow worked my way back to it. But the tables were all empty, and the banner hanging up didn't just say WELCOME, like the one upstairs.

It said WELCOME *ZED*!

As soon as I saw it, I knew that I was in trouble. I froze where I stood and couldn't move a muscle. I was in danger – but there was nothing I could do.

'*So, Zed, we meet again*,' a voice said.

I couldn't see anyone at first. As far as I could tell, I was alone. But then the shadows shifted at the far end of the room, and a man stepped into view. He was hard to make out, because he was dressed in black and looked like a waiter. But then he stepped out of the shadows, and I saw his face.

He was Dr Katterfelto.

I must have cried his name, because he took a bow. I'd thought I'd got away from him, but I'd been mistaken. Down the long miles of river valleys and hidden gorges he had followed me, waiting for this moment. Every time I'd caught a hint of something in the wind, he'd been there. And he was here too, waiting in the shadows, biding his time.

And now that time had come. All around me, other shadows started shifting, and I felt myself begin to shake all over. 'Pull yourself together, boy,' said Dr Katterfelto. 'Have a bit of dignity. Stop quivering, and stand up straight. The time has come to answer for your life of crime. And to answer properly – *no escape this time!*'

He sounded like a policeman making an arrest.

Sounded like a judge, in a court of law. I remembered my mother's words about getting into real trouble one day. And now that day was here!

Dr Katterfelto crossed the room and climbed on to a long, low dais, taking up a position centre-stage. He clapped his white-gloved hands, and men and women emerged from the shadows dressed in cocktail frocks and bow ties, just like the guests upstairs – except that these guests all wore masks. They filled the tables until none was empty. Then Dr Katterfelto clapped again and, as if he was the undisputed master of this place, as well as of all those village halls and palaces, the guests sat down.

I was left alone in the middle of the floor, standing before them all, not knowing who they were behind their masks. It was the strangest feeling being there like that. It was as if the world upstairs no longer existed. And it wasn't because I'd been hypnotised, this time. No, this was *real*. As real as anything could ever be.

Suddenly I felt angry. Despite what I'd to Gilda, I knew this wasn't fair. It wasn't justice. It didn't feel right. Dr Katterfelto had no warrant to detain me. No warrant to lure me here, and play games with me – and certainly no warrant to finish me off.

For that was exactly what he intended to do! There were no two ways about it – Dr Katterfelto was planning something terrible. And he had the means to do it, too! After all, he was a Doctor of Conjuring. He could stuff me into a cabinet and make me vanish, bit by bit. Or saw me in half. Or say a magic word and make me go up in a puff of smoke. And I wouldn't come back like Gilda had done when he'd wrapped his cloak around her. I'd be lost for ever.

'Who d'you think you are?' I burst out in a panic. 'Just because of what I did to Gilda, you can't do what you like! You've got no right. We're not in court. You're not my judge. You're just some trumped-up showman, full of tricks. I'm out of here – *and you can't stop me!*'

I was wrong. I started across the floor, heading for the door but, before I could take more than a couple of steps, I found my way blocked. A circle of dogs stepped out of the shadows and positioned themselves around me as if this *was* a court, no matter what I said, and they were its lieutenants.

I recognised them immediately – recognised the *Cŵn y Wbir.* And every time I'd looked behind me on the journey, feeling as if I was being followed, I'd been right. I turned back to the dais. The doctor looked at me with eyes as cold as curses. Eyes that I had seen before – and *then I knew.*

'No!' I whispered. '*You can't be.*'

The doctor smiled. And I had seen that smile as well. Had bowed before its power, and promised anything to save my sister. Anything at all – even my own life.

And deals were deals. There was no getting out of them.

'*You're the red judge,*' I said.

24

UNMASKED

He didn't move a muscle. Didn't as much as blink. But I was right. Everything about him shouted it – and how I'd ever thought he was a common conjuror, known by the stage name Dr Katterfelto, I couldn't imagine. I should have realised from the start. Should have known from the first trick that there was more to him than met the eye.

A rustle ran round the room, as if this *was* a court after all, and everyone was waiting. Then, at last, the red judge made his move. He took off the Dr Katterfelto costume and donned a judge's wig and red cloak of office, then stood before us all, utterly transformed. Every eye was on him, and you could see he relished the attention. A devil of a smile played around his lips, arrogant and pitying, as if he and I had struck a deal and it was time for me to pay the price.

I was the biggest fool alive. I'd thought that I could get away from him – could trick him and run rings round him – but I was wrong. The game was up.

The red judge sat down and spread his cloak around him. He called the first witness to take the stand and immediately three little giggling Barbie-girls leapt to their feet as if they simply couldn't wait, and tried to speak all at once. Even before they pulled off their masks, I knew they were my Fitztalbot cousins. I stared at them in astonishment, thinking that I might have spent a lifetime winding them up, but I hadn't done anything bad enough to warrant a court of law.

But that's not how they saw it.

'He tied me to a tree and shot arrows at me.'

'He did that to me too, and they covered me in bruises, even though they were only rubber.'

'He shut me in a cupboard and locked the door.'

'He did that to me too – and he put sellotape over my mouth.'

'He took my favourite doll and set it on fire, then he said it wasn't him but nobody believed him. He made me give him sweets, or else he'd pull out my hair.'

'He did that to me too – and he took my *Tammy-Girl* annual and threw it in the pond.'

'He tried to push me in the pond. And he made me walk across the weir, or else he said he'd tell my mother what my real grades were in school.'

'He bought us rubbish presents every Christmas.'

'He was always bullying us.'

'He was always teasing, but it wasn't in fun.'

'We hated him.'

'He was stupid.'

'He was in the way.'

'Nobody wanted him. Nobody in the family.'

'He made all our lives a misery.'

Finally they ran out of things to say – three little cousins full of highly exaggerated memories, as far as I was concerned, getting back at me at long last. Most of their complaints went back years, and I wanted to laugh at them for still remembering. But no one else was laughing. I also wanted to point out that there were two sides to every story, and that they hadn't been so terrific themselves.

But perhaps they had a case. Perhaps having me for a cousin was worse than I'd realised. In any case, I never got the chance to speak up. The girls returned to their seats and my father's younger brother and sister, Uncle George and Aunt Decima, rose to their feet and plunged into some ghastly story, pulling off their masks to tell the court about trust funds and family money, and plots to seize the family assets and cuckoos in nests.

I didn't get the half of it, but they ended with the phrase *something of the night about him*, and it stuck in my mind, partly because I'd heard it before, but I couldn't remember where – on the telly, or somewhere like that – and partly because, by the time the trial was over, it had turned into something of a theme.

I was a dark character, apparently. My deeds weren't those of any ordinary boy. One by one, my Fitztalbot relatives stood to say the same things. The masks came off, and the tongues were loosened and they couldn't stop. All of them were there, right down to the second cousins twice removed who I hardly ever saw, and whose names I could never remember.

It was as if the entire family had decided to gang up on me. They were full of nasty things I'd done, many of which I couldn't even remember, and most of which weren't that bad really – or so it seemed to me. The list went on and on until only my Fitztalbot grandmother seemed to be left. She took off her mask and stood before the court, ramrod-straight, every inch the proud matriarch, her cheeks drawn in as if she was sucking lemon drops, her eyes fixed on me with visible contempt. I could tell that she'd been waiting a long time for this.

'In your own time,' the red judge said, as if she needed special consideration because she was an old woman.

But my Fitztalbot grandmother had never needed anyone's consideration – and neither did she need permission. She was the mother of the family. The one in charge. The one whose words were law.

'My son gave that ungrateful child a home,' she boomed forth, making sure that everyone could hear. 'He gave him everything a fatherless child, living in some back-of-beyond village with nothing but a primitive education to look forward to, could ever want. He gave him a whole life – and what did he get in return? He got insolence, that's what! He got trouble and strife, and everything thrown back in his face.

'My son's a man of standing, looked up to by everybody and generous to a fault. All he asked for out of life was to have a son to carry on the family name. And this is what he got! This ungrateful boy who couldn't even do his sums, and got expelled from his old school, and ran amok around the town and continually brought shame on the family name. And *he's* the one to carry it on. The only boy amongst the lot of us – *God help us all!*'

She stopped. My aunts wilted visibly, as if this failure to produce a son was all their fault. But it was at me that my Grandmother Fitztalbot was looking, not them. For a moment, I thought that she was going to lay into me personally, but then – as if she'd said more than enough already – she stomped back to her table, sweeping past the others with such force that tablecloths shot off and glasses and candlesticks went flying in every direction.

For a moment, there was chaos in the court, everybody scrambling to pick things up. But then the red judge called for order, clapping his white-gloved hands and declaring that he had an important piece of evidence to bring before the court. His voice, as he made this announcement, was so grave that the atmosphere immediately changed.

The whole room fell silent. Then the red judge clapped his hands again, and a reel of film flickered into life on the wall above the dais. For some reason, it ran backwards rather than forwards, so that the first thing we saw was my shocked and terrified figure shooting backwards up the drive of Clockvine House. Then we saw Gilda Katterfelto lying in the snow, covered in blood. Then we saw her rising like the dead in resurrection and something big and black flying off her head and hurtling back through the air until it came into contact with my hand.

We saw my arm draw back, and the thing was a mallet. Then we saw it fly back to its hook on the wall and me backing towards it. Then, finally, we saw my face in close-up, all twisted and contorted. But we never found out why, because that was where the reel ended.

For a moment there was silence in the court. Then a woman rose slowly to her feet. I'd noticed her earlier, sitting at a table set for two, apart from everybody else. Now she took off her mask, and I saw that she was my mother. Her cheeks flamed with the embarrassment of having borne a son like me. I tried to catch her eye, but she looked away from me. I don't think I ever saw her looking more beautiful. Her hair was perfect, and so was her dress, as if she'd spent hours getting ready for the occasion.

My Fitztalbot father rose to his feet as well, lending his support by holding her hand. 'No one will ever know how I have suffered,' she said in a low voice, 'and what it's cost me to bring my son into the Fitztalbot family. If I'd only left him with his grandmother in Wales, perhaps things might have worked out differently. But I wanted the best for him, and for his sister too. I wanted to give them every opportunity. And Cary was a good girl – everybody loved her, right from the start. But Zachary ...'

She broke off, unable to carry on. Immediately my Fitztalbot father took over, ready with the words that she couldn't bring herself to say.

'Zachary was ungrateful,' he said. 'He never took the opportunities that we offered him. We sent him to the best schools, but he didn't even try. All he ever did was pay us back with bad behaviour. And now he's gone too far. We've had enough of him. We're overwhelmed with shame. There's nothing we can say in his defence. He's a hopeless case, but we're not to blame. He's not our fault. We did our best. We wash our hands of him. *He's no son of ours.*'

All round the room, you could have heard a pin

drop. Then the red judge rose to his feet, and every eye turned back to him. You could feel the atmosphere in the room becoming colder. Men reached for their jackets and women for their stoles. My mother sat down, and so did my Fitztalbot father. The case was closed – and I was done for.

'Zachary Fitztalbot,' the red judge said, looking down at me with twin fires in his eyes, burning for retribution. 'This court has heard the case against you, weighed the evidence and heard the testimonies of all the witnesses. It is now my judgement that, for bullying your cousins, for bringing dishonour to the Fitztalbot family name, for ingratitude, for insolence, for throwing your father's generosity back in his face, for bringing grief to your mother and causing her to suffer, and – most of all – *for the murder of Gilda Katterfelto*, I sentence you to ...'

I waited for it. '*Death. I sentence you to death.*' That's what my punishment would be. No other sentence would do here in the court of this judge with whom I'd struck a deal already, promising him my life. I held my breath. Prayed for deliverance, but knew there was no hope for me.

But I was wrong! In the furthest corner of the room, the shadows began to shift again and, suddenly, another figure emerged. It came striding across the floor, pushing aside the *Cŵn y Wbir* as if they were nothing but a minor hindrance. Everybody stared, including me, as an old woman in a shabby skirt and apron, her pockets full of clothes' pegs, headed for the dais. For a moment, it looked as if the court was being gatecrashed. But it was obvious the moment the woman stepped into the light, without a mask to hide behind, that she had the right to be here.

For she was my other grandmother.

Grace!

25

THE CASE FOR THE DEFENCE

Every New Year's Eve since, I've always remembered it. Wherever I am and whatever I'm doing, it always comes back to me. Sometimes I don't even have to know it's New Year's Eve and it still comes back. The whole thing's burned on my brain – the people half-risen in their seats and the expression on the red judge's face as Grace came towards him like a soul-survivor walking upon water.

She walked as if she had no fears. Nothing in this court could touch her. She wasn't even frightened of the *Cŵn y Wbir*. The red judge's legendary dogs – there to do their master's will and keep his court in order, yet they backed away as if nothing had prepared them for this furious woman.

Nor, it seemed, had it prepared their master. The closer Grace got, the more the red judge seemed to lose his grip. I don't know how she did it but, by the time she reached the dais, you could tell that she was the one in charge, not him.

And she knew it, too! She smiled triumphantly as

she passed me by, and I caught a whiff of whisky on her breath and sunshine in her hair. Caught the scent of life on her, as if not even death could keep her down. Perhaps the red judge caught it too. Perhaps that was why he sat down, looking small and beaten. And that was before Grace even started speaking.

'This court's a travesty of justice!' she cried out in a ringing tone. 'It's an insult to the law, and you, sir, are an insult to the justice system! Do you hear me? Don't just sit there looking like that. Pull yourself together. Have a bit of dignity. Stop quivering, and sit up straight! The time has come to answer for what you've done. And to answer properly – no tricks this time!'

A shiver ran round the court. The tables had been turned, and nobody could quite believe that it had happened. Grace had come back from the dead, and they couldn't believe that either. They were standing on a crossroads between life and death, but couldn't even grasp what was happening. They didn't understand.

'Make yourself comfortable,' Grace said, looking round at them all. 'Hold on to your masks, all you fine Fitztalbots – you'll need them to cover up your blushes. Then tell me what sort of people would bring a boy before a court like this? Would let him stand with no defence? With not a word on his behalf. Alone, and unprotected. Without a chance to speak for himself. What sort of family? Shame on you, I say! *Shame on you all!*'

Around the room, cries broke out. Words like 'old', 'mad' and 'troublesome' flew everywhere, with calls to 'stop her' and 'do something'. But nobody could stop Grace. Not even my Fitztalbot grandmother, whose voice rose above everybody else's.

'*And while we are about it ...*' Grace said, looking at her pointedly and shouting her down, 'what sort of grandmother would hold it against a boy because he couldn't do his sums, or wasn't grateful enough?'

Grace's eyes were blazing by now, and her words were like a whip. My Fitztalbot grandmother flinched, as if she had been stung. So did the rest of them.

'Before you start judging others,' Grace said, 'you should take a look at yourselves. This trial's a sham, and you all knew it from the start. You could have refused to go along with it, but you let it happen. You could have stopped it, but you sat back and enjoyed it as if it were the entertainment at your annual Christmas party! Well, if it's entertainment that you're after, *then watch this ...*'

I had never seen Grace like this before. Never so angry, or so powerful. She strode up to the red judge, whipped the cloak off his back and held it up for everyone to see. He tried to get it off her, but Grace shook the cloak in his face, driving him back.

'You've had your turn in the limelight,' she cried out. 'Now it's mine. Let's see what secrets you keep hidden here. What little tricks, waiting to be conjured out of thin air!'

She shook the cloak and things started falling out. First it was old pennies that had been stuck down in the lining, and then it was the lining itself, coming away in a single piece. Then a woolly mitten came flying out, followed by a matching red wool hat. Then a boot came flying out, followed by another. Then a duffle-coat came flying out – a hefty-looking duffle-coat with chunky padded lining. Then I don't exactly know *what* happened, but suddenly it wasn't a cloak hanging between Grace's hands.

It was a boy!

All around the room, people gasped. But I gasped louder than the rest because *I knew that boy!* I'd met him once before, throwing snowballs at sheep. Now I stared at him, remembering him pointing me in the wrong direction, sending me up Plynlimon when I'd asked for the main road. He'd even laughed as I set off.

But he wasn't laughing now! Grace was shaking him as if he was a wicked child in need of punishment. She shook so hard that the rest of his clothes fell off him, right down to his pants and socks. The room rang out with protests that it wasn't right to treat a child like that. But, before anyone could stop her, it wasn't a boy hanging between Grace's hands any more. He'd gone, shaken clean away – and someone else hung in his place.

It was the dad this time! The one who'd built that snow-castle, complete with towers and battlements, then gone indoors leaving me to freeze outside. He'd smiled as he'd closed his door – a strange smile, I'd thought at the time, but one that had filled me with black despair.

But he wasn't smiling now! He was being shaken as if he'd known what he was doing – known the despair he'd left me in and hadn't cared. His clothes came flying off him, just like the boy's had done. Layers of coats and scarves and hats went flying in every direction until they'd finally all gone, and so had he, and the person hanging between Grace's hands was someone else.

It was the snowplough driver this time. The one who'd carried on through the forest when the *Cŵn y Wbir* were chasing me, disappearing from sight when he could have stopped to help me. Now Grace was shaking him as well, as if she knew that he had seen me waving and yelling. She shook and shook until everything came off him and a crow appeared instead. A huge, black crow with a crabbing voice that went through me.

Then Grace shook the crow, and feathers flew everywhere, and a cat appeared. A small, black cat, just like the one that had trapped me in the stable block at Clockvine House – the one I'd tried to kill, but had killed Gilda instead.

Then Grace shook for a last time. Fur went flying everywhere and the cat screeched and clawed and tried to get away. But Grace was too strong for it. She wouldn't let go. She shook and shook. And, when she'd finished, *Gilda* hung from her hands.

Gilda Katterfelto!

I stared at her, and Gilda stared back, her eyes as bright as emeralds. The last time I'd seen her she'd been dead, but now her cheeks were full of colour, and there wasn't a hint of scar where that flying mallet had struck her. I cried out in astonishment and, all around the room, people cried out too. They didn't understand how the Gilda on the flickering film could be this Gilda now. And I didn't either – but one thing was for certain.

I had been fooled!

Gilda glanced at me, edgy and nervous, and gave a little helpless shrug as if she didn't understand either. It was then that I snapped. I mightn't know exactly what was going on, but I could tell she'd been a part of it all the way along. I leapt on to the dais, snatched her off Grace and started shaking her myself. I thought I'd never stop. Her green silk costume went flying one way and her cap the other. Her hair flew away, just like the cat's fur before it, and crow's feathers before that. Then the rest of her went too. I shook and shook until nothing – *nothing* – was left.

Finally my hands were empty. I held them up, and everything had gone. The cloak. The boy. The man. The snowplough driver. The crow. The cat. Gilda Katterfelto. Not a trace of any of them. I turned to Grace. I still didn't understand.

'It's very simple,' she said. 'Gilda wasn't real. She was an illusion. So were all the rest of them. They were pieces in a game whose purpose was to trick you and confuse you, to spur you on, string you along, outsmart and outmanoeuvre you. To see you run, and track you down and – when the fun was over and you finally became boring – do away with you.'

A buzz of voices broke out all round the room. Embarrassed voices, as if behind their masks people were finally realising what they'd got caught up in. Amid the general clamour, the red judge rose to his feet. None of the others noticed, but Grace did.

'*Go!*' she cried to me. 'Get out of here! He can't hold you. He's got no right. You didn't kill Gilda, because she didn't ever live. You may have thought you did, but that was an illusion. You're free, Zed, free! This so-called court can't touch you. Go. Right now. *While you still can!*'

I should have done it, like she said. But something made me hesitate, and then it was too late. As if he had regained his strength, the red judge clapped his hands. Immediately, a black candle flame sprang to life deep in the shadows at the outer edge of the room, revealing a hospital bed with my sister Cary lying in it. She was covered in tubes and bandages and surrounded by screens and monitors that bleeped as if her life still hung in the balance, despite what Pawl had said about her turning a corner, and only I could save her.

My mother cried out, and so did my Fitztalbot father. And I cried too, knowing that the red judge had got me. I looked at Grace, and she looked back as if she knew the deal I'd struck and couldn't help me. For a few moments there had been a chance, and she had seized it, but now that chance had gone.

The red judge smiled, holding out his hand to me, as if the game was won fair and square. And perhaps it was, and I would have shaken on it, conceding defeat. But suddenly a new voice rang out – one that I recognised, but didn't know where from.

'Cary's life is hers alone, to live and die in her own time!' it shouted. 'It isn't yours to give, or take, or gamble for or buy. She stands and falls by her own efforts, thank you very much. And so does Zed. He's capable of great things, and he'll do them too, and if some here in this room can't see it in him, then that's their loss. They may look down on him, and think he isn't good enough and even wash their hands of him. But they don't see him like I do. *Don't see him like a father looking at his son!*'

The moment was electric. Voices broke out all round the room. Then a figure came striding out of the shadows and I recognised it – of course I did. But I knew it wasn't possible. It simply couldn't be. Not so firm, and bold and certain. Not with words so clearly spoken. Not the man I'd always thought of as my uncle.

Not Pawl Pork-pie.

On the far side of the room, I heard somebody start to cry. I turned and saw that it was my mother. She was looking at Pawl as if he was somebody she'd once known, long ago, but turned her back on. Her expression was sheet-white, and there were things in it that I had never seen before. Hidden secrets, shaken out at last. Secrets between the two of them.

She said his name. 'Pawl,' she said, but he wouldn't look at her.

Instead he looked at me – my shambling uncle, who couldn't usually string his words together but had done it just this once, because he wanted people to know that he was proud of me!

'Pawl,' I said, as well. And then, because I understood at last, and wanted him to know – understood it all, and the word I'd longed to use was suddenly appropriate – I said, '*Dad*.'

Then the whole room erupted as if an explosion had taken place. Everything went flying up in the air. Somewhere in the chaos of it all, I heard Grace crying, '*Yes, oh yes!*' as if it was out at last, and my mother no longer had a hold over her. I tried to get to her, but tables went flying between us. So did my cousins, Frieda, Lottie and Claudia, along with all my other Fitztalbot relatives, and the monitors and tubes and my sister Cary's hospital bed.

Bells rang inside my head. The WELCOME ZED banner went flying past, and so did chairs and tablecloths, silver cutlery and crystal glasses. The *Cŵn y Wbir* were swept up, howling, into darkness. The black corph candle was snuffed out, as if it had lost its power, and my ramrod-straight Fitztalbot grandmother was swept away like a handful of old bones. The red judge was swept away, clutching his wig. He went flying past and the expression on his face was enough to last me a lifetime. Then he was gone, and the shadow of Plynlimon fell from me.

Finally, Grace went as well. I saw her swept up with the rest of them. And I never got to say goodbye, but I felt her brave spirit in the face of death passing down to me like a family bequest.

It took a while for the dust to settle. When it did, I found myself standing back in the hotel basement, before a staircase leading up into the light. It was the world I'd left behind, and I climbed the stairs to join it. Through the open kitchen door, I could see left-overs from the New Year's Eve dinner – everything from tureens of soup and carcasses of pheasant to the remains of lime tarts and baked chocolate pies.

Suddenly I felt hungry. It wasn't the hunger of a starving boy who'd eat berries if he really had to, but the hunger of an ordinary boy who wouldn't mind the chance to stuff his face.

'There's food upstairs ... for us waiting ... in our room,' a voice said.

I turned around, and it was Pawl. The rest of them had gone as if they'd been a dream, but he remained, as real as ever. And the room key in his hand was real as well.

26

THE OFFER

I awoke in a sea-green hotel bedroom to find myself curled up in an enormous four-poster bed with curtains pulled around it. Pawl lay at the bottom of the bed, sprawled across a chaise longue. His shoulders rose and fell as he snored his way towards morning. I sat up and watched him. I couldn't see much likeness to myself, but knew that I had found my father. My real father too – not some father I'd invented because I didn't have anybody else, but the one who'd always been there for me, even though I hadn't known it.

It felt like coming in to shore after a long sea voyage. I got out of bed, too excited to lie still, went to the bedroom window and pulled back the curtains to let in the new day. Outside the sun shone across the forest with not a hint of mist. It was a beautiful morning, crisp with snow-white frost, but as bright as summer. The light awoke Pawl. He ran his fingers through his hair, and sat up looking confused as if he didn't know how he'd got here. I'd wondered that as well, but, from the expression on his face, I guessed I mightn't ever find out.

We made ourselves cups of coffee, watched a bit of morning television, ran ourselves hot baths and finally went down for breakfast. In the dining room a table was waiting for us, with our room number on it. The waitress greeted Pawl by name, as if he was a proper signed-up guest, and we tucked into a full English breakfast, not scrimping on the toast or extra cups of tea.

Then, after we had eaten, we went out walking. I wore Pawl's old black coat, which had dried out overnight on the bedroom radiator, and he wore his pork-pie hat. I wondered what the hotel staff made of us, down there at the reception desk, me in my scruffy clothes and him with half his back to front. He checked out before we left, paying for our room with handfuls of money, then leaving the hotel abruptly without wanting change.

We made off through the forest, following the sun. I was full of questions and didn't know where to start. I wanted to ask Pawl about the red judge's court and how he'd come to be there, about my mother and their lives together and about the accident that hadn't killed my father, like I'd always been told, but had turned him into Pawl Pork-pie.

When I tried to ask, however, Pawl started looking confused again, as if he didn't know what I was on about. In the end I gave up trying and we walked in silence, drinking in the cold, crisp air. Maybe answers weren't always necessary, I told myself. Maybe, especially on days like this, it was good enough just to be alive.

We passed silver ponds, freshly frozen over in the night, and wooded copses so deep and hidden that the frost hadn't found them and neither had the sun. We climbed hills full of spruce trees, decorated with real-life Christmas baubles fashioned out of ice, passed beech trees, oak trees, ancient hollies, young, sweet chestnuts, aspens, alders, birch trees.

The list went on and on. The landscape of the forest was changing all the time. Sometimes we were in deeply wooded areas, with not a sign of human life, but other times we came across worn tracks with heavy tyre marks, and stacks of felled logs, ready for transportation. Sap oozed out of their sawn-off ends, sparkling in the sunlight like clusters of polished diamonds. I remember brushing against it, and its scent was like the perfume of the forest – something to take away with me and remember the day by, when we finally went our separate ways.

I think I always knew, right from the start, that we would end up going separate ways. I didn't say a word about it and neither did Pawl, but I think he knew it too. I remember us reaching the edge of the forest, and standing there knowing that our time had come. We'd climbed a hill and found the river on the other side, running like quicksilver through a salt marsh estuary. A town lay nestled at the bottom of the hill, and the sea sparkled in the distance. I stood looking at it all, thinking that this was as far as my journey would take me.

Then Pawl and I headed down the hill, not a word said between us. We entered the town and made our way through its streets, which were mostly empty because it was the first day of the new year. There were no buses at the bus station, or taxis in the rank outside the railway ticket office. But we walked on to the platform as if we knew the station was open really, and stood waiting for our trains to come along.

That they would, we had no doubt, even though it was a public holiday. Mine came first, and nobody got on it except for me. I slammed the door behind me, and we stood facing each other through the open window, still not a word between us. It was as if we were both afraid of spoiling the moment by saying the wrong thing. Then Pawl thrust some money at me through the open window. 'For the journey ...' he said. 'Happy New Year.'

My train pulled out, and he disappeared. The least said about that the better. After I settled down, I found a photograph amongst the handful of notes that he had given me. It was of him and my mother. He wore a white carnation in his lapel and she wore a white dress and held a bunch of flowers. She was smiling. They both were. They were very young, and both looked pretty different to the people they were now.

I sat looking at them throughout my journey back to Pengwern. Sometimes I dropped off to sleep, but they were always there, right in front of me, when I opened my eyes. By the time I reached my destination, I knew every detail of that photograph so well that I can recall it without difficulty, even now.

It must have been mid-afternoon when Pengwern's spires and rooftops finally appeared. I put away the photograph and watched the castle drawing closer as the front of the train pulled over the railway bridge. My heart started thundering. The conductor's voice informed all passengers that they should make sure not to leave any baggage behind. But I was the only person who got off the train, walking empty-handedly down the platform, head down, collar up, fearful of being recognised.

Not that I needed to worry – one look at the stranger reflected in the ticket office window and I wouldn't have recognised myself. Who was this gaunt, thin, hollow-eyed boy in his big black flapping coat? I turned away from him with a slight shudder, and set off into town, not knowing what I was doing here, and rather dreading finding out.

When I hit the main shopping streets, I found that, though I might have changed, nothing else had. The Christmas decorations were still up and the people still the same. I saw my sister's cello teacher, Mr Bytheway, on Pride Hill. But he didn't see me, and neither did our dentist, Mr Jenkins, who drove past in his car.

I turned my head away quickly, but I needn't have worried. It was as if I'd acquired the knack of invisibility, walking through the streets of Pengwern without anybody looking my way. I spent the rest of the afternoon in town, hanging around the High Street and Pride Hill, buying food and drink in the few cafés that were open, using the money that Pawl had given me.

Finally they closed and the empty streets looked like a ghost town. Not knowing what else to do, I headed for Swan Hill. Here I found a couple of our house lights on, but my parents' cars gone from the garage. Sighing with relief, because I wouldn't have to face them yet, I located the spare key, let myself in and headed through the scullery towards the back stairs.

Pengwern mightn't have changed, but our house had. Before I could get far, I quickly discovered that something was up. Boxes were stacked up everywhere, and cupboards had been emptied. Paintings had been removed from walls. Books had been removed from shelves. Statues had been wrapped up carefully and labelled. Dustsheets had been thrown over the furniture.

I went from room to room, and everything was the same. What was going on here? Down in the kitchen, my mother's pots and pans had been packed away. In the drawing room, the Christmas tree and all its decorations had been taken down. In my father's study, dustsheets had been thrown over his desk and chair, and his shelves emptied of books. In the rubbish bin I found the photographs and broken frames where I had thrown them and the bunch of mistletoe that I'd hung over my father's desk, knowing that it would irritate him.

Now I took it out, thinking how childish I had been. I've changed, I thought. I'm not the boy I used to be. No wonder I can't even recognise myself!

I turned to leave the room, but my mother stood in the doorway, car keys in her hands, a coat thrown over her shoulders. I hadn't heard her drive up, but now here she was, staring at me in surprise.

I guess I was surprised as well. We both blushed, and I can't remember what we said to each other, only that we ended up in the kitchen, drinking warm white wine because that was all my mother could find. The fact of my banishment was brushed under the carpet. My mother didn't mention it, and neither did I.

Neither did she mention anything that had come between us since, from the phone messages she'd left because she didn't want to speak to me, to the way she'd washed her hands of me in the red judge's court.

Perhaps she doesn't know about it, I thought. Perhaps it's been wiped from her memory. Or perhaps it was a dream, and never really happened. Or perhaps it *did* happen, but in another place and time and she doesn't even know that she was there. Or perhaps she does know somewhere deep inside, but she's so upset that she simply can't bear to mention it.

I wanted to ask her, just to hear what she would say. But my mother talked at me non-stop and I couldn't get a word in edgeways. It was as if she was afraid of what would happen if she stopped. She didn't mention my changed appearance, and I didn't mention it either. I was on my best behaviour, nodding like the perfect house-guest as if fascinated by the things she said.

'Did we tell you that we're staying at your Fitztalbot grandmother's house?' my mother said. 'At least we are until your father can make other arrangements. He wants to sell this house because he says it is unlucky. He won't come back to it, not even for a night. He's a deeply superstitious man, although you may never have realised it. Beneath his calm exterior, he's full of feelings and strange fears. He says he's always been uncomfortable living here, and we've never been happy, and he's convinced the house is cursed.'

She shrugged and smiled, as if the whole thing was ridiculous, but what could you do? People make their own curses, I thought. They curse themselves – and they take their curses with them when they move.

But I didn't get the chance to say so, for suddenly my mother was on her feet, declaring that she had to go and pulling on her coat. She looked round at all the boxes piled up everywhere, and you could see from her face that she was deeply afraid. Her old life was crumbling away, and she was over the abyss and in free-fall – *and I knew how that felt!*

What I might have said or done, spurred on by fellow feeling, I'll never know. Maybe I would have given her another chance – shown her the photograph and asked her if there was anything she wanted to tell me – but the phone rang and it was my Fitztalbot father wanting to know how long she'd be.

'I'm just coming now. Yes, right away. I've got your books – I haven't forgotten them. Of course I've remembered to turn off the lights. See you soon. Goodbye. Yes. Yes. Of course. Love you, too.'

It struck a sad note, that word of love hanging in the air with nothing to cling on to. I looked at my mother, and she looked at me. 'Your grandmother serves dinner at seven-thirty,' she said. 'You can have a lift with me if you want to eat.'

Then she turned towards the door and I knew that, never mind the dinner, I was being offered back my old life, no apologies asked for and certainly none given. It wasn't much, but it was all my mother had to give.

I took a deep breath. Swallowed hard. 'Thanks, but I'm not hungry. I think I'll pass,' I said.

27

PHAZE II

My mother would never know what my refusal cost me – nor what it would have cost if I'd answered *yes*. After she had gone, I went from room to room one final time. A strange silence seemed to follow me around. I ended up in the kitchen again, standing at the table on my own, staring at the empty wine glasses, thinking nothing in particular. Finally I left, banging the front door behind me, knowing that I'd never come back.

I went up to the hospital, which was what I should have done in the first place, to find out about Cary. By the time I got there, however, visiting time was over. I took the lift to Intensive Care, but my sister wasn't there. The main lights were out and the corridors were empty. Occasionally nurses could be seen trailing between beds or sitting at lonely desks. I've no idea how they failed to see a late-night visitor creeping through the shadows, but I went right through the hospital and nobody noticed me.

Finally I found Cary in a private ward, which,

knowing our father, is where I should have looked first. Her name was on the door and I slipped inside. With thick pile carpets, flowers on a plinth, leather armchairs and a telly, it could have been a hotel bedroom. I tiptoed to the bed and looked down at Cary's face against the pillow. Her eyes were closed and a little scrub of hair was growing back. I could see the scar where the light bulb had been glued to her head, but the bulb itself had gone.

The monitors had gone as well, and so had most of the tubes. I remembered what Pawl had said about the fight being Cary's, and hers alone.

'*Well done*,' I whispered.

Immediately, Cary's eyes opened, as if I'd woken her. She looked at me and neither of us spoke. I knew that she recognised me, even if I scarcely recognised myself. I also knew that, in the morning, she'd tell herself I'd been a ghost, come to say goodbye. She'd think that I had died sometime over Christmas, lost in a blizzard on Plynlimon Mountain. My father would think so too, and even my mother would think it, despite the evidence of her own eyes. She'd convince herself that she'd never really seen me at Swan Hill tonight, but had imagined it. Either that or, like Cary, she'd think I'd been a ghost.

My sister fell back to sleep, her eyes closed again and a little smile around her lips. I dug down in my pocket and pulled out the photograph of our parents on their wedding day, which I propped up by her bed where she'd see it first thing in the morning. Then I left the room, knowing that this was the real reason why I'd come back to Pengwern.

Outside the hospital, with nothing left to keep me

here, I walked back to the railway station. I'd catch the first train out, I decided. Buy a ticket with the remains of Pawl's money, and get as far away as possible.

When I arrived, however, I found the station locked for the night, all the platforms empty and not a hint of a train in sight. Unable to think of anywhere else to go, I squeezed in through a side gate that had been left unpadlocked, and found myself a night's shelter in a boarded-up building at the end of all the platforms, behind a row of advertising hoardings.

The smell that greeted me in there was rank, but it was warmer than outside, and at least I'd be ready to catch the first train in the morning. I pushed my way back into the darkness, looking for a corner to curl up for the night. But the building went back further than I anticipated, and it was darker too. As soon as I dropped the board back over the window, I was lost. I couldn't find any walls. Couldn't find any corners. Couldn't even find the window any more, in order to get back out.

I stumbled through the darkness, but it went on and on. All hopes of finding somewhere that felt safe enough to sleep quickly faded. Sometimes I fell down steps. Sometimes I hit my head. Sometimes I thought I saw lights, but then realised that I hadn't. Sometimes I heard noises too – rumbling noises that I couldn't figure out, and scuffling noises, as if I shared the darkness with rats and mice.

Finally I found myself on a ledge with water running under it. I could hear the sound of pigeons overhead, and make out what definitely looked like lights in the distance. At first I couldn't figure out what those lights might be but, as I worked my way towards them, I realised that I could see moonlight reflected in the river.

I carried on until I could see stars reflected too, and streetlights and even house lights. It was if I'd stumbled upon a mirror image of the whole town. I stood looking down at it all, realising that I'd somehow worked my way into the underbelly of the railway bridge. The river flowed away beneath me, and the town rose overhead until it reached the spires and castle walls that formed its skyline.

I stayed awake all night, looking at that skyline and the moon above it, caught in a limbo-land between the bridge and the town, and my old life and a new one. I sat on a girder, my legs swinging over the edge, watching the river flowing out of sight, and remembering that day when I'd come up here to spray a zed. Then I'd wished, against all odds, that I could shake off being a Fitztalbot.

And now I had.

I sat there until morning, wondering who I'd like to be instead. The sun rose. The streetlights went off. The moon waned over the castle and morning broke in the sky over the English Bridge. I thought of all the things that had happened to me. Some made sense, but some were still a mystery. There were questions that I couldn't answer, and didn't know if I ever would.

But one thing was for certain.

There really *was* a red judge's court, I thought. And I really *was* on trial for my life. I didn't just imagine it in some state of crazed exhaustion. I really did cross swords with the Red Judge of Plynlimon. And I really did defeat him. *At least for now.*

I shivered at the thought of him out there still, maybe plotting his revenge, maybe looking for another victim. But that was someone else's story, not mine. The time had come to put the past aside. My life was on the turn. It was changing, like the moon over the castle, passing from one phase to the next.

Finally I pulled my coat around me, and struggled to my feet. It was time to go. I should have felt excited, but all I felt was sad and lonely. People passed beneath me on the river path, never looking up – cyclists on their way to work and early-morning walkers with their dogs, all with lives to live and homes to go to.

But what did I have?

In the end, scarcely knowing what I was doing, I drew myself a map. I drew it inside my head because I didn't have a pen, and put Plynlimon at the top and the sea at the bottom, with the two rivers flowing into it – the Afon Gwy and the Sabrina Fludde. Then, as if the rivers marked the boundaries of my memory, I drew in my whole journey.

Everything was on it, from Swan Hill to Clockvine House, Plynlimon Mountain to the Speech House Hotel. And there were people on it too. Grace and Pawl. Cary and my mother. The red judge as himself, and in the guise of Dr Katterfelto. And Gilda was there, even though she wasn't real. And the Fitztalbots were there too, even though I'd rather not remember them. And the boy bishop was there, and the seven strange sisters who'd healed me by turning scummy river water into wine. And the man in Llewellyn's Cave was there – the one I'd thought must be a pilgrim, but who could have been anyone, even Prince Llewellyn himself.

All of them were there, and the creatures too. I drew in the *Cŵn y Wbir* because, as with the Fitztalbots, my story wasn't complete without them. And I drew in Harri and Mari in memory of a friendship that I swore I'd never forget.

Finally the map was finished. My whole story, mapped out in my head so that I'd never forget it, whatever happened next. And that's the story I'm telling you now. Maybe it's getting rusty and its finer details are beginning to fade. But everything that matters is still there. And I'm there too – drawn in with the rest of them because the map is big enough for everything.

You can even find my name on it, if you know where to look. Not my old one, Zachary Fitztalbot, because that boy has gone, and so has that old life. But the name I chose that morning, standing on the girders facing daybreak over Pengwern.

Phaze II – spelt with a zed.

Pauline Fisk

Pauline Fisk grew up in London, but has spent most of her life in Shropshire. She started making up stories for her friends and neighbours at the age of three and made her big career decision to become a professional writer at the age of nine. She has five grown-up children, an architect husband and a dog. She loves living in Shropshire, which she thinks is the most beautiful county in England, with some of the most interesting legends and history.

Pauline Fisk wrote *The Red Judge* as a companion novel to *Sabrina Fludde*, drawing on the legends, history and modern life of two of Plynlimon Mountain's great rivers, the Severn and the Wye.

'*The Red Judge* grew out of my fascination with legends and history,' says Pauline, 'and with the way that the past, the present and the future connect. It's a story about homelessness, and what it means to belong, and about discovering a rootedness that comes from within oneself. It's also a mystery about a magic mountain and its secrets and it's about the age-old battle between good and evil.'

www.bloomsbury.com/paulinefisk

By the same author